After All These Years
The Cedarville Series #7
By
Bree Kraemer

After All These Years

The Cedarville Series
Bree Kraemer
Published by Bree Kraemer, 2020.

This is a work of fiction. Similarities to real people, places, or events
are entirely coincidental.
After All These Years

Third edition. March 31, 2020.

He's A Keeper
Ground Rule
Walk Off
Sacrifice Bunt
Grand Slam (Coming soon)

Chapter 1

Wes might have bitten off more than he could chew and while a few years ago he would have thrown in the towel and chalked it all up to a bad decision, this time was different. This was his dream and he wasn't going to let a little hard work stop him from getting what he'd always wanted.

He was almost ready to open his restaurant, Dockside. Two more days and it would be open for business.

Somehow, someway, construction had stayed on schedule and in just two days, Dockside would be open and he'd have customers. Hopefully. He'd originally wanted to open before Memorial Day weekend but his brother, Dax, had told him right away that was impossible. But two weeks later wasn't so bad.

Plus, had he been open for Memorial Day, he would not have been able to help Carly and Tony by catering their wedding, and the feedback he was getting from guests about his food was phenomenal. Not to mention people saying they would definitely come back to the restaurant.

Dockside had been a staple in Cedarville for as long as he could remember. But it had gone downhill over the years until finally, it closed. When Wes had found out that the owner was interested in selling, he jumped at the chance. And thanks to the help of Dax and his friends, he was able to renovate it cheaply for his mid-June opening.

It was weird living back in Cedarville again after being away for so long. But leaving had been a no brainer. There was no way he could have continued to live in the town and get cleaned up. Getting clean from drugs was hard enough, but having the whole town watch would have been harder. So he'd moved to Columbus and worked hard at becoming drug-free. It had been ten years, and not only was he drug-free, but he was about to open a business.

Talk about crazy.

Tonight he was having a soft opening for his friends and family. Well, to be fair it was his family and their friends. Sure, he knew some of them, but he wasn't sure he would call them his friends. At least not yet. But thanks to Dax and his girlfriend, Avery, they were all willing to help out whenever needed.

That was one of the things he'd missed about small-town living. The way everyone was willing to pitch in when they needed help.

He liked all of Dax's friends, a lot. Interestingly enough, Dax himself had only been friends with them for a few months. But like Wes, he'd known most of them his whole life. Or at least known of them.

Like the Grahams.

Brandon, Logan and Carly were all part of the Graham family and they were staples in Cedarville. Not to mention, Brandon was the chief of police, and Logan was a famous photographer who everyone knew, even if they didn't live in Cedarville.

They were all coming to the soft opening along with their spouses or partners. Plus a few more, including a few of the guys who worked for Dax, and Avery's sister, Joy, who also happened to be his new roommate.

A week ago he concluded that he'd had his fill of living with Dax and Avery. He loved them and Dax's house was plenty big enough for the three of them.

Or so he'd thought.

One night he left his room at two in the morning to get a drink of water and walked in on them defiling the island countertop. Needless to say, that was his cue to move out and to also never eat or cook on that counter again.

Joy, who like him was the black sheep of her family, mentioned that she was looking for a roommate. When he'd first met Joy, he'd taken to her right away. Not in a sexual, dating way, but in a little sister or best friend way. They just got along well. So after the incident on the counter, he'd asked her about moving in. She'd agreed, and within a day, he had his stuff moved in his new place.

As a bonus, it was only two blocks from his new restaurant.

He was straightening chairs and tables when his new bartender, Sabrina, came in. Sabrina had applied for the head bartender job along with six other people. She'd won out though because the girl was a beast. She could take orders, mix drinks and calculate tabs all at the same time. Wes had been a bartender for ten years and she was even better than he was.

"Hey," she said, as she bypassed him and went behind the counter.

The only thing about her was that she wasn't much of a talker unless she was working. Behind the bar she chatted up the customers no problem. But other than that, she rarely spoke, and when she did, it was only if it was important.

Small talk was not her thing.

He'd hired six more staffers who would both serve and work the bar if needed. He would do all the cooking, at least for now. If it ever got to the point where it was too much, he would hire more staff.

"The bar should be all stocked," he said, as he dropped his dishrag that he'd been using to wipe down tables, in the sink.

She nodded. "Anything I need to know?"

"Nope, I think you're covered. Just remember that tonight we are only charging cost for the alcohol and the list is taped right there." He pointed to the list that he'd attached to the cash register.

She nodded again.

Leaving her, he pushed open the door that divided the bar from the kitchen. His guests would have the option of a full menu tonight because he wanted to make sure he was capable of handling it if things got busy. It wasn't a large menu anyway. Sandwiches, burgers, grilled chicken, but there were a few specialty items. Mac and cheese that he made from scratch, and a jambalaya that everyone who ever tasted it, loved.

Plus, he made his fries from scratch meaning that each day he'd have to peel enough potatoes to cover the orders. He was hoping that he'd be able to teach someone on staff how to do it, when and if, they had downtime.

He began warming up his burners and making sure everything was organized when his brother walked in.

"Are you ready for this?"

"Too late if I'm not, right?"

"This place looks fantastic. I can't believe we got it finished so fast."

"I wouldn't have been able to do it without you." It was true too. Dax had worked for free in all his spare time to help him get the place ready.

"You're my brother, what was I going to do, let you fail?"

"You could have but I'm glad you didn't. Is Avery with you?"

"She's out there chatting with Sabrina."

Wes lifted an eyebrow. "My bartender? Sabrina? The one who never talks?"

Dax laughed. "It seems that Avery has made it her mission to make her open up." He put his hands up. "Don't ask me, man. I don't question Avery."

"As long as she doesn't quit, I don't give a damn." They walked out of the kitchen together, and sure enough, Avery and Sabrina were talking.

"Oh, Wes, this place looks fantastic!" Avery shouted. "I've been so busy the last few days that I haven't had a chance to stop by and see the finished product." She walked up to him and gave him a hug. "I'm so happy for you."

"Thanks, Avery." He looked around. "It did turn out pretty good."

He heard the front door open and turned to find Tony and Carly coming in, along with Addison and Ryan.

"I guess I should mingle, at least until I have to go cook." He walked toward the newcomers. "Hey, guys, thanks for coming."

"We wouldn't miss it," Tony said, and shook his hand. "It's the least we can do for the man that saved our asses at our wedding."

Tony and Carly had just gotten back from their honeymoon, and it showed. They were both tanned and relaxed.

"Hit the bar for drinks if you want, or just have a seat anywhere. Your server will take your order as soon as you're ready."

He left them and then greeted a few more people. Once people started to sit, he moved back to the kitchen so he could be ready when orders started coming in. For over an hour he cooked, fried and stirred. When the last order was filled, he pulled off his apron and hairnet, ran a hand through his short hair, and went back out front. As soon as he stepped through the door, applause rang out.

He was overwhelmed but nodded and smiled. What else could he do?

"Man that was delicious," Brandon said to him. "I can't think when I've had better jambalaya."

"And my grilled chicken was perfect," his girlfriend, Leah, said. "Not everyone does chicken right."

He graciously smiled and thanked them. It was weird having people praise him, but he was going to have to get used to it if he wanted his restaurant to be successful.

He went around the bar and poured himself a glass of water. He wasn't a big drinker, even though alcohol wasn't his drug of choice back when he was using. But he still tried to live a clean life by not drinking regularly.

For a few years, after he went through rehab, he drank. But after a while he made the decision to stop. He had a fear of relapsing that was strong enough to make him stop.

He mingled with his guests for a while longer until they all began to trickle out. He sent all his servers home including Sabrina, and soon it was just him, Dax and Avery sitting around a table.

"You really did it, bro."

"The food was amazing," Avery said. "I might have to eat here every night."

"If you do, it's on the house."

"Don't tell her that," Dax said, "or she really will be here every night."

"You guys helped me make this place, so feeding you is not a big deal."

"You can't run your business like that." Avery gave him a look that reminded him of the ones his mom would give him when he was a kid. "Rule number one, no free food."

He laughed and shrugged. "If you say so."

"Really though," Dax said, "this place is going to do well. I can feel it."

"I hope so. I've put everything I have into it so if it fails I'm screwed."

"You won't fail," Avery said. "I won't let you. If I have to drag people here kicking and screaming I will."

Dax took a drink of his beer. "How's living with Joy? You know, you really didn't have to move out."

"Yeah, I did. You two need your space and I never want to see what I saw on that counter again. Please tell me you disinfected?"

"Oh my God, stop being a baby," Avery squeaked. "It was just sex and since you're not a sixteen-year-old virgin you need to get over it. People have sex."

"But not usually on the counter in their kitchen."

"I know several people who have done just that."

He looked at Avery and then at his brother. "You're awfully quiet over there."

"I'm just biding my time until you are in a relationship and then I want you to tell me that there's no way you would have counter sex."

"You're going to be waiting a long time because I have no desire to be in a relationship." Been there, done that, he thought to himself. Sex was one thing, but a relationship was not something he ever wanted again.

His brother smirked. "Good luck with that."

Wes rolled his eyes at his brother's comment as Avery said, "Cedarville will have other plans for you. No one makes it out of here without finding true love."

He groaned and pushed back from the table to stand. "All right. You've overstayed your welcome."

"We'll leave," Avery said, "but just know that when we get home, that counter might just get defiled again." She gave him a hug and then they left.

Locking the door behind them, he leaned back against it and closed his eyes.

He'd done it. He'd actually had a successful first night. Sure it had been his family and friends but that didn't matter. They'd all liked the food and his servers had done well and felt comfortable.

He officially owned a restaurant.

For a minute he thought he might hyperventilate.

People were going to rely on him for their livelihood. He couldn't let them down or the town that had worked so hard to back him. This had to work.

It would work.

The next day, he was back in the restaurant making sure the docks were ready for boats. This was the one part of the job he was concerned about. He hadn't hired anyone to deal with the docking, figuring that everyone could do it themselves like they had with the previous owner. He did have some outside seating but it was all plastic tables and chairs, so nothing that he had to be overly concerned with. One of the servers would take care of the outside customers if and when they came.

After a few hours at his soon to be home away from home, he headed to the apartment that he shared with Joy. This was his last night off for who knows how long, so they were planning on hanging out and maybe watching a movie.

As soon as he walked in the door, he knew she was home. He liked her, he really did, and they got along great except for one thing. She was as messy, as messy could be. It drove him up the wall.

And since he had cleaned that morning and now the living room was a mess, she absolutely had to be home. His suspicions were confirmed when she walked out of her room and greeted him.

"Done for the day? I thought for sure you'd flake on me and stay there all night."

"A promise is a promise." He automatically started cleaning up, a habit he couldn't help.

"Sorry I was asleep last night when you got home but it was a long day at the salon." Joy was a nail tech and worked at a salon in Woodridge currently. She was looking to work locally but so far no one was hiring.

"Tell me the truth, was the food okay?" She'd been his guinea pig more than once over the last month so he trusted her. She didn't hesitate to tell him if something didn't taste good.

"I had the mac and cheese and a burger and both were fantastic. And your bartender...that girl knows how to make a drink." She came into the kitchen with him and leaned against the counter. "Everyone I talked to said they enjoyed their food."

He gave a sigh of relief. "Sometimes I still can't wrap my head around the fact that I am cooking food and people are going to be buying it. It boggles my mind."

"You deserve it. You've worked hard to get here. I'm hoping someday that will be me."

"Your own salon isn't that far off, and now with me living here, you are saving more money each month. It'll happen."

She rolled her eyes like she always did when they talked about her and changed the subject. "So pizza tonight?"

"Yup. I'll order it and you go pick the movie." She started to walk away. "But no chick flicks!" he yelled after her.

She was in a self-imposed dating slump and liked to say that since she couldn't date she liked to watch the movies about people falling in love.

He wasn't sure why everyone wanted to fall in love. Being single was pretty awesome, at least as far as he was concerned. He could do whatever he wanted without having to answer to anyone. Whenever he and Dax were together, Dax had to call or text Avery to make sure it was okay. And sure Wes went to bed alone, while Dax got to snuggle up next to a warm, beautiful woman who loved him, but that wasn't a big deal.

He got to hog the whole bed and didn't have to worry about anyone stealing the covers.

That was the dream.

Right?

Shaking himself out of his thoughts, he quickly ordered the pizza. Half meat for her and half veggie for him. While he tried to take care of his body, she ate as much bad food as possible. Not to mention the candy. She was like a five-year-old with how much candy she ate. She once told him she ate the candy as a substitute for sex.

He was thinking maybe he needed to try it.

He found her already on the couch, knees pulled up under her butt. "All right, what's it going to be?" He sat down and stretched his legs out in front of him on the ottoman.

"What about Lord of the Rings?"

"Works for me."

She started the movie and as they watched, they each made comments about characters or things that happened. They had both seen the movie, more than once, but this was what they did. It was one of the reasons they got along so well.

He knew that when they'd first hit it off, Avery had wished that they'd get together as more than friends. But that just wasn't how it was.

There was only one woman who Wes had ever loved and when she broke his heart, it was permanently.

Chapter 2

Making sure her mom was settled, Julia went back to the kitchen where a glass of wine was waiting for her. She didn't normally drink alone. No that wasn't right, up until three months ago, she absolutely did drink alone. But now she had friends – or at least a friend – and she didn't need to drink alone anymore.

But just like two nights ago, Avery was at Dockside for dinner, and because she was persona non grata, it was just her and a bottle of chardonnay.

She didn't know for sure that she was persona non grata at Dockside, but she assumed she was, since the owner and chef was none other than her ex-boyfriend who she'd left high and dry when he'd needed her the most.

The main reason for why she'd left.

They were the perfect high school couple or so everyone said. Wes had been everything to her. Together they'd fallen in love and been each other's first in every way that mattered. First kiss, first sexual experience, first love.

And she couldn't forget, first drug experience.

They'd experimented together, wanting to just try it and see what the big deal was. And for a while it was fun and innocent. Until it wasn't. They'd started with pot and eventually they tried cocaine. That had been their downfall.

When she'd had enough and decided to stop, Wes wasn't ready yet. For a while she'd stayed with him trying hard to get him to go see someone to try and stop. But soon it had become too much for her to handle and leaving was her only option.

She'd had an offer at a school in Tennessee, and instead of waiting around for Wes to clean up, she left.

Just upped and left.

When he'd needed her.

It was the worst moment of her life.

Taking a giant gulp of her wine, she closed her eyes and pictured a young Wes Lange.

He'd had dark, shaggy hair and chocolate brown eyes that she'd get lost in if she looked at them too long. He'd been skinny back then but not scrawny. More tall and lean. And his smile was always so genuine. Everyone had liked him, and it was because that damn smile never failed to put people at ease.

He should have become the therapist.

Instead she had. That wasn't always what she'd wanted to do, but after dealing with his drug problem, she wanted to help people. And she was good at it. At least she hoped.

When her dad had died last year, her mom begged her to move back. How did you say no to that? Her parent's were the definition of love and losing her dad had practically killed her mom. Not wanting to be a shitty daughter, she picked up her practice and moved it to Ohio.

To the same town she'd grown up in and where she'd fallen in love with Wes.

To the town that watched as they fell apart.

To the town he wasn't supposed to be living in...she'd checked a dozen times before moving home.

But then three months ago, she met Avery, and found out that not only was Avery dating Wes's brother Dax, but that Wes was moving home and opening a restaurant.

She wanted to find the biggest hole and bury herself in it.

Except that in three months, she'd yet to run into him. Hell, she'd not even seen him. Not even from behind. And she'd looked. Many, many times.

She knew from Avery that Wes was busy at the restaurant and, because she had no reason to go to that side of town, there was no chance of running into him there.

When she and Avery hung out it was either at her mom's house – yes she was a thirty-four-year-old woman who owned her own medical practice and still lived with her mother – or at a bar or restaurant. Avery knew the story behind her and Wes, so she made sure to keep them apart.

Well Avery knew part of the story.

No one except she and Wes knew the whole thing.

Draining the rest of her wine, she decided one glass was enough and went to mope on the couch. She hated that she was the lone one out. Avery and Dax, along with all the other people Avery had introduced her to, were all at Dockside for opening night. Leaving her to sit alone and play Scrabble with her mom.

She loved her mom, really she did. But hanging out with her on a Friday night was not her idea of fun. It had been over a year, but now she wanted a life. A life with friends and dates and...just people.

Dropping her head back against the couch, she sighed. Maybe it was time to start dating. Several doctors at the hospital had asked her out but she'd always said no. At first she'd turned them down because of her mom and needing to spend her extra time with her. But recently, it was because she knew Wes was in town.

But it wasn't like she and Wes were anything to each other, right? Why shouldn't she date? When she'd lived in Tennessee she dated. Well kinda. If going out with a guy once or twice, then having sex and being done, was considered dating.

It wasn't that she was averse to dating, it was more that all the guys who wanted to date her weren't...well, they weren't Wes, if she was being honest.

She'd been ruined at sixteen for any other guy by having the perfect first boyfriend.

How does that happen? She should be able to get over him and move on. Hell, she was a fucking therapist. She worked through these kinds of things every day with her patients.

Maybe it was like that old saying, *those who can't do, teach*. Only for her it was *those can't date, help other people date.*

Not that those were the only people she helped. Some of her patients had drug problems and some marital problems and some were just stressed. But a good amount liked to talk about love and the best way to find it.

Only, she was no expert.

Finding the remote, she flipped on the TV and searched for something to watch. Settling on some mind-numbing reality show, she let her eyes close as she tried to picture what an adult Wes looked like.

She was just getting to the good part – his naked chest – when her phone rang. Seeing that it was Avery she answered with, "I thought you were busy?"

"I was, but now I'm not, and Leah and I are on our way over, so break out the wine."

"You're coming here?" Not that she minded but she'd assumed they would be busy all night.

"Yeah, so turn off the stupid TV show and be ready. We'll be there in a couple minutes."

Avery hung up without even saying goodbye and Julia just stared at the phone. She was elated that Avery and Leah were coming over. Of all of Avery's friends, she had taken to Leah the most. They got along well and had a similar sense of humor. Not that she didn't love the other women, but there was just something about Leah.

Turning off the TV, she went into the kitchen to make sure she had wine chilling. She still had the half-open bottle she'd been drinking from earlier, but she added a second to the refrigerator, in case they needed it. Once that was done, she walked to the front of the house so her friends didn't knock. Her mom was a heavy sleeper and would likely not wake, but she didn't want to take the chance.

It was just after nine, so it was still kinda light outside. Stepping out onto the porch, she watched as Leah's car pulled into the driveway.

Both Leah and Avery got out of the car and walked toward her.

"Is your mom already asleep?" Avery asked.

"Yeah, but we won't wake her, so don't worry." They knew the drill since they'd both been there before while her mom was asleep.

They all went inside and gathered around the kitchen table.

"I'm surprised to see you guys," she said as she grabbed three wine glasses. "I thought you would stay later?"

"The place was packed so we bailed figuring that would give them more space," Leah said. "Addison and Ryan went home too, and so did Mel, Logan, Carly, and Tony."

She wanted to ask how it was, but since this had to do with Wes, she stayed quiet.

"What's up with you?" Leah asked. "I feel like I haven't seen you in awhile."

The last time she'd seen them was right after Carly and Tony's wedding when they'd gone out to dinner. "I've been busy. I had a new set of rehab patients last week and I do those hours at night after my regular patients. It's draining but worth it if I can reach even one of them."

"You're so impressive," Avery said. "The work you do really helps people. That has to feel good."

"It has its moments." She shrugged and took a sip of her wine. Wanting the conversation off her and onto something else she asked, "How is Addison doing after the big surprise wedding? I still can't believe they got married at Carly and Tony's wedding."

Because she was new friends with them, she hadn't been invited and that was fine, but when she'd found out that Addison and Ryan had an impromptu wedding the same day, she'd been bummed. Addison's wedding had been one she was looking forward to attending.

"Addison is over the moon about both the wedding and the baby," Avery said. "Ryan is like a love sick puppy at work without her there. It's funny but also cute. I hope that's the way Dax is when I'm not around."

"He is, don't worry," Leah said and rolled her eyes. "I was at Carly and Tony's the other day while Dax was there measuring for their remodel, and when Carly said your name, a goofy, glazed look crossed his face. Tony had to say his name three times to bring him back to reality. It was sickening."

"Oh don't even act like Brandon isn't just like that," Avery said. "That man is so smitten with you that he won't even let you open a car door. Like you'll break a nail or something."

Julia listened to their banter, laughing at funny comments but wishing she had something to contribute.

"What about you," Leah asked, "are you dating anyone?"

"Funny you should ask that. I was just thinking that it's time to get back in the game."

"Anyone in mind for this game?" Avery asked.

"Not yet, but several of the doctors at the hospital have asked me out."

"Why didn't you go out with them?" Leah asked.

She shrugged. "When I moved home it was because my mom needed me. I wasn't going to just up and leave her night after night. But now, she's doing better and I can have a night or two away."

"Would you ever move back to Tennessee now that your mom doesn't need you?" Avery asked.

"I've thought about that but decided against it. If I want to be successful in my practice, I can't keep moving it. So I'm here, it seems, for the long haul.

"I, for one, am glad," Avery said. "I'd hate to lose a friend."

"Me too," Leah added. "We need all the woman power we can get with all the testosterone the guys put out."

"I'm glad I met you guys. If not for you, I'd be wallowing in my wine watching bad reality television."

"I like reality TV as much as the next girl," Avery said, "but we're young and should be out having fun. Believe me, I wasted too many years sitting at home when I could have been out having fun."

"Maybe you're young," Julia said, "but I'm thirty-four." She groaned. "How'd I get to be thirty-four? And worse, how am I still single?"

"Beats me," Leah said. "First, you don't look thirty-four and second, have you looked in the mirror? You have natural bedroom eyes. I bet you don't even wear mascara."

"You'd be wrong and I don't know what bedroom eyes are?"

"Bedroom eyes are when you always look like you're ready for sex," Avery said. "Which is why I have no idea why you aren't in a relationship. Guys have to be lining up around the block to date you."

"Ha! As if." She sipped her wine and wondered if she really did have bedroom eyes.

"I have an idea," Leah said. "Next week at work, pick a guy who has asked you out before and say yes."

"What, I'm just supposed to walk up to him and say I've changed my mind?"

"Yes," both Avery and Leah said with Leah adding, "It'll work, I promise."

She frowned. "I'll sound like an idiot. Plus I don't like any of those guys."

"It doesn't matter," Avery said. "You aren't going to marry them, you're just using them to get some dating experience."

"And to find out what you like and don't like," Leah said.

"Like and don't like in bed? There is no way I am sleeping with any of them." Just the thought made her want to vomit.

She'd been with guys since Wes. Hello, that was fourteen years ago. But it had been at least three years since she'd had sex. The only thing that went near her vagina was her vibrator, which was somehow, coincidentally, named Wes.

Oh good Lord, she was in trouble.

"No, dummy," Avery said. "I mean if you want to sleep with them, sure go ahead and do it. But, we mean try them out, as in see what you like and don't like in a guy."

She knew what she liked and didn't like.

Likes: Wes.

Dislikes: Anyone who wasn't Wes.

It was a pretty simple list.

"Why do I get the feeling she already knows what she likes?" Leah said to Avery.

"Probably because you are a smart woman." Avery turned to her. "Do you want to talk about him?"

Avery knew the bare bones of her relationship with Wes and when they had become friends she'd made her promise that they'd never discuss him. But now, she wasn't so sure she wanted that. Maybe talking about him would help.

"Is it stupid that it's been fourteen years and yet I still miss him?"

"That's not stupid at all," Leah said. "When you love someone it can take time."

"But fourteen years? Come on, that's longer than some dogs live."

"He doesn't date either," Avery said quietly.

She whipped her head around so fast she almost gave herself whiplash. "How do you know that?"

"I overheard him talking to Dax one night. Right after he got clean, dating wasn't on his radar. And then later, he did date a little but nothing felt right."

She swallowed the lump in her throat. There were so many questions she wanted to ask but the first one that popped out of her mouth was, "What does he look like?"

"I can handle this," Leah said and picked up her phone. Flipping through photos, she found the one she wanted and turned her phone toward Julia.

And there he was.

Wes.

Her Wes.

His hair was shorter than it had been back in high school but his eyes, they were the same.

"I saw a few high school pictures of him," Avery said, "and from what I can tell, he's put on some weight, most of it muscle. He works out all the time, or he did before when he first moved to town, and since he eats clean and doesn't really drink, he's pretty fit."

Julia couldn't take her eyes off the photo. It had obviously been taken at Carly and Tony's wedding from the background. But what struck her the most was his smile. It was the same.

"You know, he asked me about you once?"

She swung her eyes up to Avery. "What did he ask?"

"He wanted to know if you were happy."

"What did you tell him?" She felt like she was going to hyperventilate while waiting for the answer.

"That I wasn't sure." Avery shrugged. "It was the truth then, and still is."

She dropped the phone and slid it back over to Leah. "I had a chance at happiness once but I screwed it up."

"From what I know, Wes is the one who screwed it up, Julia. You couldn't be expected to stay with a person when they wouldn't get clean. That wouldn't have been good for you."

"Avery's right," Leah said. "Love can only take you so far, but if the person isn't willing to help themselves, you can't be faulted for leaving."

She pushed back from the table. "You guys don't know the whole story." Standing, she paced the small kitchen.

"Then tell us," Avery said.

She looked at her two new friends and debated spilling her guts but she just couldn't. She was a fucking hypocrite if there ever was one. "I just can't." She sat back down. "Thanks for talking with me about him. It might not seem like it, but it helped."

"Anytime," Leah said. "Now, are you coming to my house next Saturday for the cookout?'

Leah and Brandon were having a big cookout at their place for all their friends. She'd been invited but wasn't sure if she planned to go because she didn't want to be the only single person there. "Are any other non-couples coming?"

"As a matter of fact, yes," Leah said. "One of the guys who works with Dax, Flynn, I think his name is, and also Avery's sister, Joy. Plus possibly a few more."

"All right, if you're sure." She'd met Joy once before and liked her. She was different from Avery, more colorful. Hopefully a few other singles would show up.

They spent another hour at her house telling stories and chatting. After they left, she locked up and headed to bed. Right as she laid down, her phone dinged with a message, picking it up, she saw it was from Leah. Opening it up, she gasped when she saw it was the photo of Wes that Leah had shown her earlier.

There was no message, just the photo. She didn't have any words to thank Leah, so she didn't reply. Saving the photo to her albums, she turned off the light and brought the phone closer to her face.

He was breathtakingly handsome as a grown man where as a teenage boy he'd been merely cute.

She ached to run her fingers through his hair and have his eyes light up like they used to. But she knew that would never happen.

But dreaming about it was okay, or at least she hoped it was.

She felt her eyes swell with tears at the life she could have had if only she'd given him more time. She didn't bother to wipe them away and instead let them fall.

For months after she'd left town, she'd cried every night. But it had been years since she'd let herself cry over what could have been. Maybe this was what she needed to finally move on.

Or maybe not.

Either way, it was cathartic and she wasn't going to hold it in any longer.

Chapter 3

Wes was overwhelmed.

So many people had come out to show their support of his restaurant, and not only that, they'd come back a second or third time. He'd been open a week already and he'd seen several of the same people.

He wasn't even open on Mondays, at least not right now. He figured that was the easiest day to close where people wouldn't miss him too much. Every other day, he opened at eleven for lunch. During the week he closed at ten and on Fridays and Saturdays closed at midnight. Those hours would change during the Winter but Summer on the lake was always a busy time.

He'd been packed both for lunch and dinner all week, enough so that he was already thinking about hiring more people. He knew in the winter things would change, but while the lake was busy, it seemed like he would need more help.

He was going to look for high school students or maybe college students that needed a summer job. Those would be the best so that he wouldn't feel bad if he had to let them go at the end of summer.

It was already three o'clock on Friday and they had a small break between the dinner and lunch crowds. Sabrina was cleaning down the bar while he swept the floor.

"Have tips been good?" he asked her.

"Better than I expected."

"Good." He continued to sweep. When he finished, he stored the broom in the closet and went out on the dock to make sure everything was set. As he straightened tables and chairs, a boat pulled up and docked.

Looking out to the lake, he saw that it was Logan.

"Hey, man, you not working today?"

"I worked this morning but then decided to blow off work for the afternoon. Thought I'd come by and grab a meal."

"Sure, come on in." They walked inside and Logan took a seat at the bar ordering a soda from Sabrina. "Know what you want or do you need a menu?"

"I'll take a burger and fries."

"Coming right up." Wes went back to the kitchen and grilled up the burger and threw on some fries. While the burger cooked, he plated the lettuce, tomato and onion along with a pickle spear. Once the burger and fries were cooked, he added them and walked out to the bar.

"Here ya go, man."

"Thanks. How's business been?"

"Better than I could have predicted. Honestly I'm a little shocked."

"Why? People used to come here all the time before it went downhill. This town has needed another casual restaurant for a while, so I am not at all surprised."

"I just hope it lasts." He walked behind the bar to grab himself a glass of water. "Hey, you wouldn't know of any high school or college kids that might need a job would you?"

"I don't but I can ask mom. She knows everything."

"I'd appreciate that. How's the wedding planning going?" Logan and Melanie were getting married in the middle of September which was only a couple months away.

"Not bad. Melanie has it all covered and my only job was to hire a photographer."

"And let me guess, you haven't found anyone yet?" Logan was a world-renowned photographer himself so, Wes could only imagine how hard it was to find someone he liked.

"Actually, I called in a favor to a friend and he is coming into town to do it for me." The words were happy but his voice was dull.

"Why do you not sound happy about that?"

"In exchange, I promised to go with him on a week-long photoshoot in early November. I hate traveling."

While Wes had been gone from town for a while he did know about Logan and his career. "Wasn't it not that long ago that you were galavanting all over the world?"

"Don't remind me." He picked up a fry and dropped it in his mouth. "Now that I have Melanie, I don't want to travel unless it's with her."

"I don't think a week will kill you."

"That's right, you don't have a girlfriend so you don't know what regular sex is like. Not to mention just sleeping in the same bed with the woman you love." He smiled. "There's nothing better. Not even Fiji."

Wes rolled his eyes. "The men in this town have all gone insane."

Logan's grin got even bigger. "You don't know what you're missing."

Wes left him to finish his food and went back to the kitchen. A few more people had come in and he had orders to cook.

From then on out, he was busy. There was no time for a break and that was okay with him. No break meant the place was busy and busy meant he was making money.

Nothing wrong with that.

When one of his servers came back and told him that they'd closed for the night, he finally looked at the time. It was just after eleven. They still had a few customers left who were eating, but no more food would be ordered.

After he cleaned the kitchen and organized for the next day, he went out front to help. He was surprised to find that his staff had finished cleaning and it was just him and Sabrina left.

"Wow, you guys worked fast."

"They're hard workers." She kept cleaning the bar, but looked up at him. "You're going to need to come up with something for dessert. People keep asking."

"I know." He wasn't a baker. And honestly didn't have the time to deal with it. "I'll start looking into it."

"I might know of someone."

"Yeah?"

"I have a friend and she bakes on the side but is trying to make a go of it full time."

"Set up a time for me to meet her. You know my schedule."

They closed up and once she was gone, he locked the door and headed home. Walking in the door to his apartment, he found Joy still awake.

"No early appointments?" he asked.

"Nothing until eleven, which is good, because I worked twelve hours today and my fingers and hands are cramping."

He knew nothing about manicures and pedicures but from what Avery had told him, Joy was the best at what she did. So good, that salons all over requested her. Which was why she worked as a contractor and not an official employee of any one salon.

"How was business tonight?"

"Busy." He moved to sit on the couch and opened the bag of food he'd purchased on the way home. "So busy that I forgot to eat." Which was why he was eating fast food at midnight. He hated fast food but it had been the only thing open.

"I was wondering if hell had frozen over."

"Pretty close." If he had to eat fast food, at least the place had salads. "Are you going to that thing at Brandon and Leah's tomorrow?"

"Yeah, against my will. Avery says I have to come."

"You should go. I'd go if I wasn't working."

"You're so lucky."

"Stop being a hermit. You gotta get out and live."

"You sound like Avery. Why do I have to live? I lived enough the last few years to last for a lifetime."

Joy had gone through a bad spot where she'd hooked up with guys just for the sake of hooking up. Reality hit when her sister had been attacked by a guy who thought Avery was Joy.

"We talked about that, Joy. That's in the past and now you have to live in the present."

"Yeah, yeah blah, blah, blah. You two are like a broken record."

He ate the rest of his salad as they watched late-night TV. Joy started to get tired, leaving him to go to bed. He wanted to sleep, knew that he needed it after the long day he'd had. But he couldn't quiet his head.

Only it wasn't restaurant stuff that was buzzing around in there. It was relationship stuff.

He hadn't been lying every time he'd said he didn't want a relationship. He'd been there and it had practically ruined him when it ended.

Julia.

The only person he'd ever loved.

Why, after fourteen years, could he not get her out of his head? She'd shown how much she'd cared for him when she left. That should have been it. He'd gotten clean on his own, he'd worked his way back to a hard-working person on his own, and he'd opened a business on his own.

He'd proven that he didn't need her.

Only...he did need her.

Or at least he wanted her.

She was the only one who could make him feel better with just a look. The only one who even fourteen years later, made him crave. And she was the only one his heart would ever belong to.

He hated it.

He should despise her. She'd left him when he'd needed her the most. Not only that but she was to blame.

No, no. She wasn't. He, and only he, was to blame for his drug addiction. His therapist had made him say that over and over again throughout the years.

He had made the choice to use and he had made the choice to continue to use.

Nothing else mattered.

Obviously, because if it did, he'd be able to get over her instead of pining for her years after they'd broken up.

He'd tried dating and found that he compared each and every one of the women to Julia. And sex, yeah that had been a disaster.

Not that he hadn't still done it.

He was a guy who thought he'd never have a second chance with his one true love. It was only normal to look for connections elsewhere.

Until three months ago when he'd moved back to Cedarville. After only being in town a few days, he'd heard that Julia was also back in town, and from then on, no one else measured up.

But that didn't mean that he wanted her back.

Did it?

She'd wrecked him. Literally, torn his heart from his body.

Only a sick masochist would still love her.

He sighed and dropped his head back against the couch. It looked like he was a masochist after all because he could not stop thinking about her.

He'd seen her once. From across the street. To be fair he'd driven to the hospital and sat outside until he saw her go in. He'd had to see her. Couldn't not.

As a teenager, she'd been pretty with her long brownish hair with blond streaks and her skin tanned from days on the lake. Her eyes were huge and smokey all on their own with no make-up involved. But, when he'd seen her that day walking into the hospital, what he saw only made his heart ache more.

She was gorgeous as an adult. Her hair was shorter and darker with none of those blond streaks. Her body, which had been skinny, was now curvy all over and his hands had itched to touch her. He hadn't been able to see her eyes since she wore sunglasses, but he knew they were the same.

That was something that couldn't change.

He'd felt like a pervert watching her walk that day, but it also helped him come to a conclusion.

He still loved her.

And it wasn't going anywhere.

Now he just had to decide what he wanted to do about that.

When he walked into Dockside the next day, he found Sabrina already there along with a young woman who was sitting at the bar talking to her.

"Wes," Sabrina said. "I'd like you to meet my friend, Dani. She is the one I was telling you about." At his quizzical look she added, "The baker."

"Oh yeah, I'm so sorry." He held out his hand to shake hers. "I'm Wes Lange, it's nice to meet you."

"Thank you for taking the time to meet with me."

"Why don't we go sit at a table and talk?"

"Sure." She picked up two plastic carrying cases, one circular and one rectangular.

He lowered two chairs to the floor and they each took a seat. She pulled a sheet of paper from her back and slid it across to him. "I know nothing on there is bakery related but that's because I do this on the side. I did add a list of references at the bottom of clients I have baked for."

"Dani, relax." Like Sabrina, she was young. A quick glance at her resume and a little math, showed her to be twenty-three. "Tell me about yourself."

"Well, right now I'm working as a receptionist for an accountant in Woodridge. I went to community college and got my associates degree but never went any further because all I've ever really wanted to do was bake, and I figured school wouldn't help with that."

She spoke fast and he wasn't sure if it was nerves or excitement. "What do you bake?"

Her eyes lit up. "Oh a little bit of everything. I brought an apple pie and also some cupcakes."

"Why don't I try a little bit." He lifted his head to ask Sabrina to bring him a plate, fork and knife but she was already there.

She set them down without a word and then walked away.

"I'll try the pie first."

She lifted the lid of the circular container and began to cut him a small piece. "It's really better warm and with ice cream but this will have to do."

He took a small bite and was immediately blown away. It was decadent and melted in his mouth. "Holy shit, that is amazing," he said around the bite. Once he swallowed he said, "Sorry about the language but that was fantastic."

A giant smile covered her face. "You really like it?"

"Like is not the word." He wasn't a person who ate sweets but maybe he was missing out.

"Try a cupcake now." She slid one onto his plate. It was decorated simply, but after taking a small bite, he realized there was nothing simple about it. The icing was caramel and maybe vanilla, and the cake was chocolate and creamy and moist.

For a second he closed his eyes and savored it. It had been too long since he'd indulged in anything that was bad for him. Maybe he needed to change that.

"That was delicious," he finally said.

She looked relieved. "I brought some other flavors if you'd like to try those?"

He held up a hand. "I've seen—or tasted—everything I need to. I'll order desserts from you."

"Oh my gosh, really?"

"Absolutely. These will sell like hotcakes. The only question is how many can I get a day?"

"I can make several dozen cupcakes a day but probably only two or three pies. I just don't have the oven space for more."

"Why don't we start with twenty-four cupcakes and mix them up any way you want, just make sure you label them and then two pies. Again your choice. Once we see what sells, we'll go from there."

"You don't know what this means to me."

They worked out the details including price and when she would deliver. She'd insisted that he keep the ones she'd already made and, because he didn't feel right not paying her for them, he took out his wallet and gave her some money.

"Cute kid," he said to Sabrina when she was gone.

"She's not a kid. She's the same age as me."

"Yeah but you're like an eighty-year-old ex-marine in a twenty-something body. She's green and naive."

She nodded. "I'll accept that assessment of both her and me."

"Thanks for bringing her in. I think the customers are going to be very happy."

"Hey, Wes," she said as he started to walk away. "Thank you for hiring her. She needs this."

He was shocked to see that Sabrina seemingly cared for someone. That was the first time he'd seen her show emotion.

He nodded and headed back to the kitchen, desserts in hand.

He had no doubt that the desserts would sell. The question was, would Dani be able to keep up with demand?

Chapter 4

When she pulled up to Brandon and Leah's house, there were already several cars parked in the driveway. Julia grabbed her bag which held a bottle of wine, chips and her homemade salsa along with her swimming things, then headed out back. She knew the party was on the deck and lake so she didn't bother going to the front door.

"Hey," Carly said, when she spotted her. "Good to see you!" A tanned Carly gave her a hug.

"Look at you all tan."

"I know, isn't it great? Living on a lake is great but there's never enough time to spend in the sun. A honeymoon, however, is all sun all the time. Well, except for the times when we were definitely not in the sun."

Julia laughed. "Yeah, I'm pretty sure that honeymoons are supposed to be more about the lack of sun times versus the time in the sun."

"Don't worry, we had lots of those."

They walked onto the deck and Julia set her chips and salsa on the table along with her wine. Then she set her bag down in the corner.

"Wine?" Leah walked up to her holding out a glass.

"Yes, thank you." She took a sip. "There's a lot of people here." She looked around at the people covering the yard, deck and dock.

"It's a good turnout. We were going to do it for the Fourth of July but decided that would be too much for a yearly thing."

"Sounds cool." Someone jumped into the water and the splash made them turn toward the lake. "Looks like someone is having fun."

Leah rolled her eyes. "Guys are such idiots sometimes."

Julia knew that from first-hand experience. "Is Avery here yet?"

"Right here," she said, coming up behind her. When Julia turned she found not only Avery but also her sister, Joy. "You remember, Joy right?"

"I do. It's nice to see you again."

"You too. Where can I get a glass of that wine?'

"Coming right up," Leah said.

"Joy, a colleague of mine at the hospital mentioned you the other day. She said you gave her the best manicure she'd ever had. She was telling everyone to go see you."

"Was it Kara?"

"It was."

"That explains why I've been so busy lately. I think she must have taken an ad out in the newspaper or something. I've been swamped."

"That's good, right?" Avery said.

"Oh definitely. It just makes for long days."

"I bet," Julia said. "Do your hands cramp?"

"Yes. Badly. I was just telling Wes that last night. Twelve-hour days are not my friend."

"W-wes," she stuttered out. Why had she seen Wes at the end of her day?

"Yeah, I was shockingly still wide awake when he got home last night. It was weird, as tired as I was, I had all this extra energy."

Julia knew she was still talking but she didn't hear any of the words after *he got home*. Were Joy and Wes in a relationship?

"Julia," she heard Avery say her name. "Wes and Joy are roommates. He moved in with her a couple of weeks ago to get out of our hair."

She looked at her friend. "Roommates?"

"Just roommates."

"Did I miss something?" Joy asked, looking between her and Avery.

"Julia and Wes…" she trailed off and Julia could tell she wasn't sure what to say.

"We used to date. A long time ago. Back in high school." She tried to play it off as if it was no big deal but even to her own ears it didn't sound that way.

"We're seriously just friends. I promise. He's like my brother. Not that I have a brother but he's what I would assume a brother would be like."

"I don't... he and I aren't..." She couldn't seem to finish a sentence.

"Julia sit down," Leah said and practically pushed her into a chair.

"It's fine," she said, with no real emotion behind it.

Joy knelt in front of her. "I didn't know it was you. He's never said your name."

"He talks about me?" She had wanted to vomit but now she wasn't so sure.

"He's talked a couple of times about the person he used to love."

"Does he hate me?" She hated to sound so needy and desperate but anything to do with Wes made her that way.

"I'm not totally sure I should answer that." She looked at Avery and Leah. "He's my friend too and I'm not sure I should get in the middle."

Julia took a deep breath. As much as she wanted to know what Wes said or hadn't said about her, she admired Joy's loyalty. "You're a good friend to him. I'm glad he has you." She looked at Avery. "And you too. He needs people. That was always something he didn't have."

"Just know that if you tell me something about him, I will keep that to myself too. You're my friend too or at least I hope we're friends?"

"We are friends and I appreciate that."

"Are you good now?" Avery asked.

"I'm good. I promise." She took a drink of her wine. "Let's go have fun. This is a party after all."

Avery stayed with her for the next thirty minutes until Julia forced her to leave her side. She had just finished talking to Addison when Joy came up and grabbed her arm.

"Talk to me and walk." She was pulling her in the direction of the dock.

"Are we hiding from someone?"

"Yes." Her voice got lower. "Have you met Flynn?"

"Tall guy with the beard?"

"Yeah that's him. There's something about the way he watches me that freaks me out."

"Freaks you out or creeps you out?"

"Freaks. He's not creepy. Far from it."

"Why do you think he freaks you out?"

"This isn't a therapy session doc so don't analyze me."

"Sorry, bad habit." They kept walking closer to the dock.

"It's fine, and to answer your question, I have no idea. All I know is that when he is around, my palms sweat and my pulse races."

"That's attraction."

Joy looked at her and rolled her eyes. "I know that dammit, what I don't know is why. He is not my type."

Julia turned her head to find Flynn in her side view. He was good looking in that lumberjack sort of way. Although he wasn't wearing flannel. Actually he wasn't wearing much of anything. He only had on swim trunks, his chest bare and tanned.

Maybe lumberjacks were the way to go.

"Stop ogling him." Joy elbowed her in the side.

"I'm not sure what your type is but that guy is easily the type for ninety-nine percent of women. Men too."

"I'm on a guy sabbatical. Attraction or not, I am not doing anything about it."

"You're stronger than me. If a guy looked at me like that, well let's just say I wouldn't be standing here talking to you."

"How is he looking at me?"

"Like it's Thanksgiving and you're pumpkin pie."

Joy's eyes glassed over. "I love pumpkin pie."

"I'm thinking Flynn does too." Julia didn't know why Joy was on a guy sabbatical but she wanted to try and help. "Want a little free advice? Don't stop living just because you've made a few mistakes. You might miss something important."

Joy pursed her lips like she wanted to say something but instead stayed quiet.

"If you ever want to talk, just as friends, I am a good listener."

"Maybe another day. For now, what do you say we go swimming? He probably won't follow me out there."

Julia laughed. "I wouldn't bet on it but we might as well swim anyway."

It felt good to laugh and have fun with friends. Julia was glad she had come and was planning on enjoying the rest of her day.

Monday dawned and after her third patient of the day, she had a break and went for a walk around the hospital. She was hoping to run into Evan who was one of the doctors who had asked her out. Of all of them, he was the one who she liked the most as a person. So maybe it could turn into something.

She wasn't hopeful but felt like she should follow Leah and Avery's advice and just put herself out there. She needed to take back some power over her own life.

She found Evan in the lounge. "Hey, Julia, how are you today?"

"Good. I had a break so I thought I'd come find you." She tried to stay calm and keep her voice steady. She was so bad at this.

"You were looking for me?"

"Yeah I was wondering if you, maybe, still wanted to go out?"

"Absolutely." His blue eyes gleamed. "I'm not sure what brought on your change of heart but I'm not going to question it."

"Is tomorrow good?" she asked. The sooner the better, at least for her.

"Tomorrow is perfect. Text me your address and I'll pick you up at seven."

She left the lounge feeling pretty confident. She'd actually gone up to a guy and asked him out. Now she just had to figure out a way to make it through the date.

Ugh.

A date.

Sure Evan was nice and cute but was he someone she wanted to spend a couple of hours with at a restaurant? What would they even talk about?

Groaning, she made it back to her office for her next patient.

Riding high on nerves she somehow made it through the day and the next. She was dressed and ready to go with a few minutes to spare. She had chosen white capri pants and a green off the shoulder top. Remembering that Even wasn't overly tall, she went with flats so she wouldn't end up taller than him.

She'd told her mom about her date and asked that she please stay in her room while he picked her up. That was not something she wanted to deal with in minute one of the date.

When she heard the knock on the door, she grabbed her purse and took a deep breath before opening the door.

"Hi." He was also dressed casually in shorts and a polo. A look down showed her that he was wearing dress shoes. With shorts. It took everything in her not to groan out loud. Who wore dress shoes with shorts?

Wes would never do that.

No, she was not going to think about Wes.

"Are you ready?" he asked.

"Definitely." Closing the door behind her, she followed him to his car, a sleek black sports car, where he opened the door for her.

Once inside, they made small talk, a lot of which centered on the hospital. She'd told him over text that he was welcome to pick the place they ate. She wasn't picky and would eat almost anything. But when he pulled up to Dockside, her breath caught and her brain blanked.

"I've heard this place is amazing. Causal but apparently it has fantastic food."

She tried to swallow but couldn't. Should she tell him they couldn't eat there or should she just deal and go with the flow? He was already out of the car and walking around to open her door so it was too late to back out.

Stepping out, she took the hand he offered. "Is this okay?" he asked.

"It's fine." She had no idea how she'd gotten words out of her mouth. "I've heard good things." Wes was the cook, so maybe she wouldn't even see him. That was possible. She hoped.

The place was packed but somehow they only had to wait a few minutes for a table. It looked like a lot of people were outside or hanging at the bar, leaving room for those who wanted to sit and eat.

She tried to take in the place. It was one hundred percent Wes. Simple decor, wood everywhere and happy.

The place was happy.

Just like Wes.

They ordered drinks and then dinner and even though she was talking to Evan, her eyes were always looking for Wes. She never knew she could multitask so well.

When they were almost finished eating, Evan stopped the waitress. "The food was delicious, anyway we could thank the chef?"

Julia's eyes went wide. "No, Evan, we don't need to bother him. That's just silly."

"I can see if he has a minute to come out," the waitress said and walked away.

Panic started to set in. Wes was going to come to her table. She was going to see him. And she was on a date. A date with a guy she didn't even like.

She worked hard to control her breathing so she wouldn't hyperventilate. She couldn't stop her eyes from being glued to the door that the waitress had gone through. The door that any second Wes could walk out of.

And then there he was.

A smile on his face as he greeted a few customers and walked toward the center of the room where they sat. She knew the moment he spotted her because his steps faltered. His smile fell but he recovered quickly and continued to walk toward them, only slower.

"Hi, I'm Wes," he said, looking only at Evan and not at her. "I was told you wanted to see me."

Evan stood. "Glad to meet you. I just wanted to let you know how great the food was."

"I'm glad you enjoyed it."

"Julia and I both did, right?" He indicated to her and she nodded because that was the only thing she could do.

His eyes bore into her and she felt like he could see all the way to her soul. Holding eye contact, he said, "That's great." Only the word great didn't sound happy, it sounded angry. "I have to get back now."

She watched him leave embarrassed that she hadn't said a word. She'd frozen up. Completely frozen up. That was her chance to say something, anything, to him after all these years and yet...nothing.

Although what could she have said? Especially with Evan sitting right there. *Oh hey Wes, I'm sorry I left you fourteen years ago when you needed me the most. Can you ever forgive me?*

Yeah that sounded stupid.

"Julia, you ready to go?" Evan saying her name pulled her out of her own thoughts.

"Uh, sure." She stood and grabbed her purse from the back of her chair.

They drove home in silence and when he parked in her driveway, he turned to her and said, "So this was a dud."

She laughed. "I'm so sorry, Evan. You're a nice guy and I thought I was ready to date but I guess I'm just not."

"It's fine, at least now we know."

"I really am sorry."

"No harm is done. And now we can be friends."

"Absolutely. Thank you again," she said as she got out. She watched him pull away as she started to walk to the door. At the last second she veered and headed for her own car. She couldn't let it end this way.

This couldn't be the way her story with Wes ended. She had to speak to him. Words actually needed to come out of her mouth.

So instead of going into the house, she was in her car and on her way to Dockside. Once there, she parked and waited. She couldn't go inside and bother him so her only option was to wait. And because it was only nine-thirty, she was going to be waiting for a while.

Chapter 5

Wes was still reeling and had no idea how he'd made it through the rest of the night.

Julia had been there. And with a guy, no less.

Was it her boyfriend? Was it serious? Why would she come when she knew he owned the place? Maybe she didn't know he owned the place.

No, that couldn't be true. She was friends with Avery and there was no way that Avery hadn't told her he was opening it back up. They didn't talk about Julia, kept her out of the conversation at all times. Avery had really taken to Julia immediately—she was amazing so why wouldn't she—and had wanted badly to be friends with her. When she'd found out that Julia and he had dated and that she was the reason he'd left town, she asked if he minded them being friends. She promised they'd never be around if he was and that she would not speak to her about him and vice versa.

He couldn't deny her a friendship that she badly wanted and needed.

That didn't mean that every time she left the house to hang with her friends, he didn't wonder about Julia and if she was going to be there.

It had become an addiction, one that was strong and more powerful than any drug he'd ever done.

To combat it, he'd spent hours upon hours working on the restaurant and any extra time, working out. He ran to stay in shape, but he found that lifting helped more with tension. Luckily, Dax had a full set of workout equipment in his basement.

But he wasn't living at Dax's anymore and it was almost midnight. He couldn't just show up there to workout and he couldn't really go for a run at this late hour.

That meant he was going to go home and have a sleepless night where all he did was think about Julia.

Fan-fucking-tastic.

When the last of his employees were gone, he hit the lights and walked out the door. He had taken two steps outside when a voice stopped him cold.

"I didn't plan to come here tonight."

He'd know that voice anywhere. She always could turn him on with just her voice. He turned and found her sitting against the building, legs stretched out in front of her.

"What are you doing here, Julia?"

She didn't stand, instead she stayed seated. "I needed you to know that none of what happened tonight was planned. By the time Evan pulled up to this place, it was too late to tell him I couldn't eat here."

"It doesn't matter. It happened and now it's over. You can go home now."

He started to walk away again and heard her shuffle to stand up.

"How are you?"

He stopped walking but didn't turn toward her. "I'm great, can't you tell."

"Wes," she said, his name coming from her mouth making him remember all the times she'd said it in the past, "we can't avoid each other. We live in the same town, have some of the same friends."

He swallowed and turned toward her. She was wearing the same thing she'd had on earlier and she looked good. Great actually. "Where's your boyfriend?" His voice was tense and held a hint of anger.

"Evan? He's not my boyfriend. Tonight was our first date. That's why I had no idea where we were going."

Not her boyfriend. First date. Those two things together meant that she didn't have a boyfriend. She was single. Had she been single for all these years? Was dating or even the thought of it as hard for her as it was for him?

"Why did you come back here?"

"I wanted to apologize for ambushing you early."

"No, why did you come back to Cedarville?"

"After my dad died my mom needed me. She was having a hard time and I didn't feel that it was right to make her face it alone."

"Your dad died?" He hadn't heard that. His mom had kept him up on what was going on in Cedarville while he was living away but never mentioned that. He knew why though. She never told him anything that had to do with Julia.

"Yeah, last January."

"I'm sorry about that. I hadn't heard." Her dad had been her world and she was the same to him. Wes had always liked and respected him.

She gave a small smile and nodded. "It wasn't unexpected but it was still hard. His cancer spread fast and we'd known for some time that he wouldn't survive."

"If you need –" He stopped because he'd almost been about to say if she needed anything she should call him. But that wasn't the relationship they had. Not anymore. He cleared his throat instead and said, "I need to get going."

"Thanks for hearing me out." She turned and started to walk but then at the last second turned back to him. "Congrats on your restaurant. This is pretty amazing."

He didn't say anything else, just watched her walk away. He glued his feet to the ground because his heart was shouting at his head to run after her. Stop her from leaving and just hold her.

The urge was so strong but he couldn't. She wasn't his, never would be again. And that decision had been hers. She'd chosen to leave fourteen years ago and he needed to get over it.

Maybe that would happen in another fourteen years.

When he saw taillights pull away from the parking lot, he knew she was gone and finally got in his own car. He was reeling from their conversation. He really was sad to hear about her dad. He'd always treated Wes like his own son and he'd known how betrayed he'd felt when he and Julia started doing drugs.

Her dad had blamed him for getting her involved and the trust he'd once had with him had been gone.

It was one of the things that finally made him get clean even if it had been two years too late. He didn't want to be a disappointment for the people who had cared about him his entire life. His mom, Dax, Julia's dad and, of course, Julia.

His mind kept replaying Julia sitting outside Dockside waiting for him. She'd taken a big risk coming to see him, knowing how they'd left things. They hadn't spoken a word in fourteen years. Not one. He assumed she thought he hated her and yet she'd still come.

The day she had come to him to tell him she was moving to Tennessee was etched in his brain as the worst day of his life. He'd screamed and yelled and she just took it all. There wasn't anything she could say and she'd known it. He'd been so angry, partly because he was strung out, and partly because he felt like he was losing a part of himself.

She'd stayed so calm, saying that she knew it was hard and probably the wrong thing to do, but that she needed to do something for herself. Something that she could be proud of and something that would make a difference.

He understood that now. He suspected that she'd become a therapist because of him. She'd always wanted to help people and not being able to fix him had been torture for her.

But he hadn't needed her to fix him. He'd just needed her to stick by him and love him.

And she hadn't been able to.

So why then, after all these years did he still love her?

That was the billion-dollar question.

It was a sleepless night and then another busy day at Dockside. He was happy for the distraction because thinking of Julia hours on end was not good for his soul.

What he really needed was to talk to his therapist but, because he was in Columbus and Wes now lived in Cedarville, that wasn't possible. The next best thing though was Dax.

In the three months that he'd been back home, he and his brother had gotten closer again. They'd been close as young kids and teenagers but once drugs came into the picture, it was a different story. And then, after, Wes had held himself back from being close. But the last thing his therapist had told him before he'd moved back was to open himself up and be honest with people.

It was time for him to start doing that.

He'd texted Dax and asked him to meet him during the lull between lunch and dinner. Only there wasn't really a lull due to the fantastic weather. But, before he had the chance to let him know not to come, he was already there.

"Dude, it's packed out there."

"I know. It's getting hard to keep up." He threw some fries in the fryer and watched the chicken he was grilling.

"I think it's safe to say you are going to need to hire some help. At least on the weekends during the summer."

"Yeah, I was hoping to wait. I didn't expect this kind of turnout every day, at least not right away."

"That's a good thing though. You're a success!"

"One week of having a packed house does not make me a success."

"Don't underestimate yourself."

"Maybe you shouldn't overestimate me."

"Always the pessimist."

Wes, plated the order and set it under the heat lamp for the server. There were currently no more orders, so he had a few moments to chat with Dax.

"I had an interesting customer last night."

"Yeah, who?"

"Julia."

Dax's face went pale. "She came in here?"

"Yeah, with a date. A date who wanted to compliment the chef."

"No fucking way. What did she say?"

"She didn't say anything. Just kept quiet and let him talk. I was only out there a few minutes."

"That's...unbelievable."

"It gets better. She was waiting for me outside when the place closed."

His mouth dropped open. "With her date?"

He laughed. "No alone. She wanted to apologize. Apparently it was a first date and they were already in the parking lot before she knew what was happening."

"That was the first time you've talked to her, right? Since you guys broke up?"

He nodded.

"Was it weird?"

"It was totally weird. There she was standing in front of me, her voice the same, her face the same, her body better, if possible, and all I could do was wonder why we weren't together."

"You do remember that this is the woman who left town as soon as you guys split up, leaving you high and dry when you needed her the most right?"

"I do, but honestly, Dax, does it really matter? She was doing what she needed to do to make something of herself. How can I fault that? I needed to get clean on my own. Did I hate her for several years after that? Yeah, absolutely. But then I learned that had I had her around, I might not have ever cleaned up. I needed to do it for me the same as she needed to leave for herself."

"You're way too zen and well adjusted. It's a little creepy."

Laughing he slapped Dax on the back. "It took years of therapy and a lot of my money to be this zen."

"So what are you going to do?"

He shrugged. "No idea. But I do know that I have to stop hating her just like I learned to stop hating myself."

"I'm sure Avery will love that. She's really taken to Julia and I know all the organizing to keep you two apart drives her insane."

A waiter came back and handed him an order, so Dax said his goodbye and headed out.

At the end of the day Wes half wished he'd walk out of the building to find Julia sitting outside again. He knew that was wishful thinking but he couldn't clear the thought from his head. At home, he laid down, exhausted from the busy weekend and yet still, sleep never came.

He tried to think of anything but her, but it was useless. She was front and center and there was no way around it. His cock was hard from this new image of her he now had.

He used to picture the slim, make-up free girl he loved when he masturbated. But not tonight and probably never again. The new, grown-up Julia was a walking wet dream. Her body, which was now filled out and perfect, was all he could think about. What did it look like under those clothes? He almost wondered if she'd gotten a boob job somewhere along the way because he would have remembered if they had been that big when they'd been together. They weren't gigantic, but under her top the other night, he could tell they were large.

Gripping his cock in hand, he ran it up and down a few times before rolling it over the tip to collect the moisture. Her curves were new and interesting to him. She'd always been fanatic about staying thin. It was one of the only things about her he'd hated. She was always talking about what she could and couldn't eat. It was obnoxious and he'd hated it. He'd thought she was beautiful and would have thought so at any size.

As evident by his current actions.

Those curves she had now looked good on her. And damn if he wasn't aching to grip those hips and drive deep inside her body.

His cock grew harder in his hand as that image of fucking her took hold. He moved his hand furiously up and down until he felt his balls tighten. When he came, he did so with a low groan of her name.

He kept his eyes closed for a few more minutes so he could continue to picture her. When the vision began to slip away he opened his eyes. Grabbing a dirty shirt, he cleaned himself up before flopping back down on the bed.

Maybe now he could get some sleep.

He woke up with a clear vision of what he needed to do.

He had to find a way to coexist with Julia. She'd been right, as much as that irritated him. Cedarville was a small town and they had a lot of the same friends. He didn't want Avery to have to worry anymore if she wanted to hang out with Julia at her own house. He didn't want to avoid going places for fear that she would be there.

That was why, at seven in the morning on his only day off, he was sitting on the stairs to the entrance of the hospital. He didn't know what time she came into work and he wasn't going to chance coming later and missing her.

If he knew her, and he was beginning to think he still did, she would be at work early. She had always been that way with school and her job. She needed to be early for everything.

Sure enough, at seven-thirty, he saw her walking through the parking lot. She stopped abruptly when she saw him.

"Wes," she said and started walking again until she was right in front of him.

"I was hoping we could talk?" He stood, putting his hands in the pockets of his cargo shorts. She was wearing dark pants that fit her a little too well and a flowered blouse that hid her amazing breasts.

"Um, sure. Do you want to come up? I don't have an appointment until nine."

He wanted to laugh at how he'd known she'd be early, but he didn't. "Yeah, that's fine with me."

He followed her up the stairs and into the elevator. Neither said anything and he could feel the tension radiating from her.

"You can relax," he said in the elevator. "I'm not here to cause problems."

She looked at him across the empty elevator. "I didn't think you were."

The elevator dinged and he followed her off and down the hall. They entered a small waiting room and then her office.

"You can take a seat if you'd like." He looked around the room as he sat on one of her chairs. There was a couch, but he didn't want to sit there and have her mistake this for a session.

"What did you want to talk about?"

She was nervous and he knew that because she was playing with a small mole on the top of her left hand. She'd always done that.

"I was hoping we could somehow find a way to put the past behind us. You were right the other night when you said we have to live in the same town. It's a small place and we have too many people in common to keep hiding."

"You can do that? Just forget the past?" Her eyebrows raised.

"I didn't say forget, I said put it behind us." He looked down at the floor. "I could never forget the past."

"Oh okay. So we put it behind and what, become friends?"

"I don't know. But I think we need to try, don't you? Avery is going to marry Dax at some point and I don't want her to ever be worried about you and me being in the same room. She deserves better than that."

"I agree. Avery is amazing and I don't ever want to put her in a weird situation. So how do we do this?"

He shrugged. "I think we just have to be civil. We were friends once and it has been fourteen years. I think we can move on and be friends again."

She was silent but her eyes never left him. "You look good. Healthy."

"Clean living will do that to a person." He'd been skinny before drugs, but while he was using he was practically all bones. "You look good too. Better if possible." He didn't know why he added the last part but he wanted her to know that to him, and probably to most guys, her new curves were an asset not a hindrance.

She laughed. "Yeah, somewhere along the way I realized that being skinny wasn't for me. It took a while and a lot of therapy but I finally like myself for who I am."

"You went to therapy?" He was shocked at that piece of information.

"Believe it or not, even therapists need fixing."

"I went too, for years. Until I moved here, actually."

"If you need someone new, I can recommend someone."

"I might but for now I am okay." He looked down again and then back up and into her eyes. "I really am sorry about your dad. I know how much he meant to you."

"He wasn't really happy with me the last year of his life but it still hurt to lose him."

He wanted to ask why he hadn't been happy with her but felt as if it wasn't his place. "Is your mom doing all right?"

"She is now. I live with her," she rolled her eyes, "crazy right. Now that she's doing better though I might start to look for my own place. How's your mom?"

"She's good. Happy to have me back in town and over the moon that my workaholic brother met a nice girl to settle down with."

She smiled a true genuine smile. "Avery really is the best."

They sat in silence for several minutes. He stood like he was going to leave but then turned back to her. "Hey, Lia." Her face showed the shock of him using the nickname that he used to use but only in private. He was a little shocked himself. It had just come out. "I tried to hate you. Did for a couple of years. Once I got clean though, I understood why you left. I still do." He shrugged. "None of it seems to matter anymore though. I'm just sick to death of missing you."

He turned and left, not giving her time to say anything. He'd done that on purpose so that she'd think about him all day. It was only fair since he'd been thinking about her since she'd shown up at his restaurant on Saturday night.

Was he an idiot for thinking that maybe, just maybe, they could have a second chance? Probably. But he didn't care. Just like he'd told her. He was just tired of missing her. Tired of being alone.

He wanted what his brother had with Avery. What most of his new friends had.

Happiness and love.

Now he just had to find a way to get it.

Chapter 6

As days went, this was one of the best she'd had in fourteen years.

Wes had come by to see her and not only that but he'd said he wanted to be friends. Friends. It was what she wanted too but she never in a million years thought he'd want the same.

What she'd done was inconceivable. So much so that even her dad had been angry with her years later when he'd found out.

But he'd called her Lia. That was the name he'd used to call her when they were alone and making love. It was only ever used then. What did it mean that he'd used it, and more importantly, how was Wes able to forgive her?

She needed to talk to somebody and soon, or she was going to combust.

Pulling out her phone she sent a group text to Addison, Avery and Leah.

Julia:

I need to talk, anyone available?

Avery:

I'm still at the office and Addison is standing right next to me. Come here.

Leah:

I'm stuck at the studio until eight. I'll call when I get home.

Grabbing her bag, she left her office and headed for town where Ryan's law office was. Avery worked there and Addison was there because she was married to Ryan and to be truthful, was always there.

Pulling up, she luckily found a parking spot right in front of the building. When she walked in she found Avery and Addison, just sitting around chatting.

"You got here fast," Avery said.

"I was leaving work when I texted." She looked around. "Is Ryan here?"

"Nah," Addison said. "He went down to the gallery to see Logan."

Taking a seat, she kicked off her shoes. "This day, as well as the two before it, have been insane."

"Do tell," Addison said. "And please tell me it's a good insane. Morning sickness is kicking my ass and I need something good to take my mind off the constant nausea."

"Did your doctor give you anything for it, because I can write you a prescription if you want?"

"She gave me something but it doesn't seem to work."

"Sorry. That happens sometimes."

"Enough about Addison and her baby issues. I have to hear about them all day long and not that I don't love you, but I need to hear about something else right now."

"Hey it's my pregnancy and I'm sick of hearing about it. Julia, please help us out and talk about anything else."

"I had a date on Saturday."

"No way!" Avery said. "You actually did it?"

"I did."

"Who was this guy and how was it?" Addison asked.

"His name was Evan, and of the guys who have asked me out recently, he was the nicest and one I have a good working relationship with."

"So how was it?" Avery asked.

"That's where it gets crazy. He took me to Dockside." Like she knew they would, both Avery and Addison went silent.

"You ate there?" Addison said.

"We did. When he pulled up it was too late to say anything and what would I have said anyway? So we went in and it was fine. Wes works in the kitchen and since the place was packed I figured I'd never see him. That is, until Evan decided he wanted to meet the chef of the fantastic food."

"He didn't!" Addison yelled.

"He did."

"Oh my God," Avery said, "this story is like better than the best reality TV ever. Keep going. What happened next?"

"Wes came out and I knew the moment he saw me because his steps faltered. But he composed himself and kept walking until he was at our table. He introduced himself and Evan raved about the food. I on the other hand, sat like a fucking stone, unable to say anything. It was not my finest moment."

"And he didn't say anything to you?" Addison asked.

"Nope. He did look at me several times but never spoke directly to me. Really, I get it though. I mean, I showed up at his place of work when we haven't spoken in fourteen years. I wouldn't speak to me either."

"So that was it?" Avery asked.

"That's not even close to being it. After Evan dropped me off, I felt like I owed Wes an explanation. So I got in my car and drove to Dockside. Then I sat outside and waited for the place to close down and for him to come out."

"You're right, Avery." Addison said, looking at her. "Who needs television when you have Julia's stories? What happened next?"

"When he finally came out, he didn't see me sitting against the building, so I blurted out something stupid about not planning on going there. He finally turned and stared at me. It was my first real look at him in years. When he greeted us during dinner, I was in such shock that I couldn't focus on what he looked like. But when he was standing in front of me, just the two of us, I had all the time to look."

"Wes is a good looking guy," Addison said. "And so fit. Have you seen him in a swimsuit? Holy shit. I love my husband, but Wes is a gorgeous man."

Avery slapped her arm. "I don't think you're helping Julia."

"No, it's fine. He is gorgeous. More so now than when he and I dated."

"So what happened next?" Avery said.

"We talked and honestly, I don't really remember what about. I said something about us needing to try and get along since we have the same friends and live in the same town. He asked why I moved home. I told him about my dad dying and he was genuinely sorry. It was all just really weird. But then – and this is seriously the crazy part – he showed up at my work this morning asking if we could talk."

"Why am I pregnant during this story?" Addison said. "This is a story that needs wine."

"We're at Ryan's office, I don't think any of us can drink."

"Not true," Avery said. "Ryan and I have a fridge in the back and he keeps it stocked with beer. But I don't need a drink, I just need the end of this story."

"Well, we went to my office and he said that he agreed with me that we need to try and be friends or at least friendly and that we should put everything in the past. When I asked if he could do that, just forget everything, he said that, no he couldn't forget but that he could put it in the past." She stood because sitting was too tame for how she felt. "'I'll get back to that in a minute but it's what he said right before he left that has me confused. First he called me by the name that he only ever called me when we had sex, Lia, and then he said he had tried to hate me but that he understood why I left and then he said – and OMG my heart almost stopped beating – that none of it mattered anymore because he was sick of missing me."

"Holy fuck," Avery swore. "I don't know what to do with any of this info."

"I'm not totally finished yet. I need to tell you a part of the story that I've only ever told three people. My therapist and my parents."

Addison reached out and took her hand. "You can tell us anything, we would never judge you."

"I wouldn't be so sure about that." She sat back down. "When we were eighteen and started doing drugs Wes wasn't the one who wanted to. It was me. I asked if he wanted to try smoking pot. Wes, being Wes, agreed because he loved me and that's what he did. Then when pot wasn't fun or new anymore, I talked him into trying something harder." She looked at both of her friends. "He became a drug addict because of me. I made him one and yet I left him when he couldn't get clean. What kind of person does that make me?"

"Oh, Julia," Avery said and reached across the desk to take her hand. "You were still a kid yourself. And Wes made his own decision. You can't blame yourself for that."

"Avery's right. Wes chose to do the drugs and he chose not to get clean when you did. That is not something that is your fault."

"It feels like it's my fault and did for years. I thought I had it under control but that was until I moved back here. As soon as I found out that Wes was back in town, all the damage I did came rushing back.

"What I don't understand is why Wes never told anyone. Why for all these years, has he continued to protect you?" Avery's lips were pursed like she was thinking.

"I don't know. For a while, after I left, I wondered if he would. But when my parents never found out or never said anything, I knew he hadn't."

"You said your parents knew though." Addison said.

"When I found out my dad was dying, I had to tell him. I couldn't keep that lie in death." She shook her head from side-to-side. "God he was angry. Angry that I let him think that Wes had been the bad guy. He loved Wes. Thought of him like his own son. And Wes, he loved my dad and I ruined it by not being honest. And now my dad is dead and Wes will never know how my dad felt about him."

"You could tell him," Addison said. "I think he'd like to hear how your dad felt."

"I guess." She bit her bottom lip. "I'm just so confused. Remember when I said Wes said he couldn't forget about our past? Why would he say that and then use my nickname and say he was sick of missing me? None of it makes sense."

"I think these are questions that only Wes can answer."

She dropped her head forward and it landed with a thud on the desk. "I hate this. I'm too old for this shit." She lifted her head. "Maybe this is life's way of telling me to get over him and finally move on."

"Maybe," Addison shrugged, "but what if it's your second chance? Are you willing to throw that away just because you don't want to ask?"

"You're going to make me face him again, aren't you?"

"I'm not making you do anything but I do think you should at least find out before you move on."

She frowned but knew Addison was right. She needed to know if there was even a sliver of a chance for them. If he said no, she'd find a way to move on.

"Is anyone hungry," Addison asked. "Because this baby is telling me it's time to eat."

"Are you waiting for Ryan?"

"I'll just text him and tell him I'm going with you to dinner."

"I'm in," Avery said. "Dax is over at Leah and Brandon's working for at least another hour."

"It's not like I have any plans," Julia said.

"Stop pouting and let's go eat." Addison stood and patted her still small stomach. "This kid is apparently starving to death."

They walked out of the office and down the block. Both Addison and Avery waved and greeted people as they walked by. Julia couldn't wait for the day that she could do the same again. As a teenager, she'd known everyone in town, but now it was different.

They walked several blocks until they stopped at a local pub that served fantastic Irish food.

"This work for everyone?" Avery said.

"Fine by me." Addison pushed past them and opened the door. "Food is food."

They were seated immediately and both Julia and Avery ordered a beer while Addison groaned and ordered water.

"Don't get me wrong, I want this baby and I will love it with all my heart, but he or she better be damn good for all the shit I have had to give up during pregnancy."

"I remember during my intern years when I had to do an OBGYN service and reading about all the things you can't have while pregnant. I was just young enough and sour enough on relationships that I swore I would never have a baby."

"Hey," Avery said slamming her hand on the table, "don't ruin pregnancy before I even get pregnant."

Addison gasped and said, "Are you trying?"

"Let's just say we aren't being super careful. I know it's fast and that we haven't been together long, but Dax is thirty-five. I don't want him to be an old man before we finally have kids."

"When it's right, it's right," Julia said. "Nobody can determine that but you."

"Sometimes I love having a therapist as a friend."

She rolled her eyes and laughed. "Wait until I tell you something you don't want to hear. You won't love it so much then."

"I'm not worried."

"Did I tell you that Tony is hiring someone to help us out in the office? Two people actually. A part-time office manager and another tech."

"Wow," Avery said, "you guys must be doing well?"

"We are but it's more so we can each have some time off. Right now, with it just being the two of us, we are always so busy. And with the baby coming, it's going to be even harder."

"Ryan mentioned that he plans to take some time off once the baby is born," Avery said. "You're pretty lucky. Not all men would do that."

"Yeah, he figures he can give people enough notice that he won't be available unless it's an emergency."

"Have you thought about what you're going to do for childcare?" Julia asked.

"We aren't totally sure yet. We are toying with the idea of a few days a week, each of us taking the baby to work. My mom has also offered to help out, so there's always that."

"Those are good options and both better than paying for a nanny," Avery said.

"Would you ever stop working?" Julia asked.

"I've thought about it but I think instead of stopping all together, maybe I will just go part-time. But not until I see how hard it is. I don't want to make the decision yet and then regret it later."

"Smart. Seems like you have it all thought out."

"I'm a planner. It's what I do. So Avery, if you are thinking baby are you also thinking wedding?"

Avery squinted and pursed her lips. "Funny thing about that. As soon as Dax finishes the job at Carly and Tony's, he and I are planning a trip where we will get married."

"What!" Addison yelled. "You're going to elope."

"Shhh," Avery said. "Yes, but you have to keep it quiet."

"You don't want a big wedding?" Julia asked.

"Not really. I just want Dax and to spend the rest of my life with him. And spending all that money just seems silly to me."

"What about Dax?"

"He's good either way but loves the thought of doing it by ourselves."

"Did he actually propose?" Addison asked.

"Not yet. He says he will but wants it to be a surprise."

Julia sat quietly and listened to her friends talk about all the good things going on in their lives. She wanted that. Had she not fucked up with Wes years ago, she would already have that. The marriage, the house and the baby.

She felt like she couldn't breathe. The room was closing in around her and she knew if she didn't get out of there she'd pass out.

She ran from the booth, leaving her friends, she was sure, staring after her. Outside it was better, but she was still breathing heavily and was lightheaded. She found a bench and sat down, putting her head between her legs.

She felt a hand on her back and looked to the side to see Avery.

It was several more long minutes before her breathing returned to normal and she could finally sit up.

"Are you okay?"

Tears swelled in her eyes. "I'm sorry, I just had to get out of there. It was all too much."

"I'm not judging you, Julia. I know as well as anyone that sometimes it just all becomes too much."

"It's all so stupid. It's been years and I functioned just fine without him until I moved back here."

"But did you though? Function fine? You had a job but did you live? Take it from someone who barely did herself, that's no way to go through life."

"How do I do that? Live?"

"I think the first step is talking to Wes again."

"How'd I know you were going to say that."

"Because you're a smart woman who has even smarter friends."

"If I'm going to do it, I need to do it now or else I'll chicken out. Can you give me his address?"

"I could but I happen to know that he is at the restaurant right now. Alone."

She took a deep breath. "Pay for my drink, will ya and tell Addison I'll talk to her later. Thanks for all the advice."

"Text me and let me know how it goes," she yelled as she began to walk away.

She wasn't far from Dockside, but she figured she should have her car just in case. So she walked back to where she'd parked it and then drove to Dockside. There was only one car in the lot, an older truck, that she assumed belonged to Wes.

Parking, she steadied herself before getting out. She was so afraid she was going to back out that she practically ran to the door. Pulling it open, she stepped in and found Wes, eyes wide standing at the bar.

"Julia, is everything okay?" The look of real concern on his face spurred her on.

"Before my dad died, I told him everything. He knew that it wasn't your fault."

He blinked at her several times. "Why would you do that?"

That was the last thing she'd expected him to say. "What do you mean why did I do that? I couldn't let him die thinking I was this perfect person or thinking that you weren't perfect."

"Goddammit, Julia!" He stomped toward her. "I never wanted him to know that."

"Why not. He hated you for thinking you were the one who got me involved."

"Yeah and that I could live with. But now you went and fucked it up."

"How did I fuck it up?"

He put his hands on his hips and glared at her. "What did he say when you told him?"

"He was angry at me. For days he wouldn't even talk to me."

"And before he died, did he ever treat you the same as before you told him?"

She saw what he was getting at. "No." She shook her head. "He was disappointed in me."

"And now he's dead and you can never change that." He turned and paced the floor. "Why couldn't you have just left well enough alone?" He turned back to face her.

"I had to do it for me, Wes. You say he died being disappointed in me, but for me, it was more about how I couldn't have lived without being disappointed in myself."

He furrowed his brow and just stared at her. Seconds ticked by and then minutes. She wasn't sure who moved first but somehow she ended up in his arms with his lips kissing hers.

She was lost in the feel of his lips against hers. It was just like she remembered, only better. His lips were demanding and took what they wanted but she didn't care. She wanted him to have everything he wanted from her.

It wasn't long before his hands were behind her back and hers were in his hair. She was overwhelmed with sensations and her body was on fire. But before she could do anything about it, his lips were gone.

"Lia, I'm so sorry." He ran his hand through his hair. "That was just...I don't know what it was."

She touched her fingers to her lips, already missing his mouth on hers. "It was years of frustration on both our parts." He was breathing heavily and his eyes were focused on her lips.

"I think it was probably more than that."

"Maybe you're right." She needed to sit before her legs gave out on her. Pulling a chair down from a table she indicated to it. "Mind if I sit?"

"Go ahead," he said and then joined her. There was awkward silence for a minute until he asked," Did you ever think about me? While you were away."

She smiled. "More than any therapist would say is normal."

"At least I wasn't alone."

"You thought about me?"

"At first I was angry but that didn't stop me from missing you. Once the anger was gone, I tried to forget you by dating a lot. When that didn't work, I realized it was useless and gave up fighting."

She played with the mole on the top of her hand. "What does this mean?"

"I don't know, but what I said this morning, that I'm sick of missing you, it's the truth. It's just too hard."

"I miss you too." She looked him directly in the eyes. "I told Avery and Addison everything."

He scrubbed his face with his hands. "You didn't have to do that."

"I did. I have to own up to my part of what happened between us, Wes. It's important to me."

"I can understand that, I just hate for people to know and blame you."

"It was years ago and we've both done well for ourselves. I don't think it's going to matter. But thank you for worrying about me. I'm still in shock that you don't hate me for leaving you like I did."

"Had you never left, who knows what would have happened. I could have dragged you down with me and then where would we have been?"

"At least we would have been together." She said it so quietly that she wasn't even sure he heard her. That is until he reached across the table and took her hand in his.

"I'd have liked to have been with you, but then I might have missed this person you became. And I think I like this person."

She stared at their conjoined hands. His thumb was running back and forth over the top of her hand. "I'm pretty boring."

"I doubt that."

She cleared her throat. "I should probably go." She started to stand but he didn't let go of her hand.

"Are you hungry? I could make us something."

She sat back down. "I don't want you to go to any trouble."

"I'd like to cook for you."

She was overwhelmed with his generosity and with how nice he was being. Although she shouldn't have been. This was the Wes she knew. He'd always been nice and sweet and helpful. "I'm starving actually. I left my dinner with Avery and Addison before I could eat."

"Great." He stood, her hand still in his. "Come on back and we can talk while I cook."

They walked hand-in-hand, which was surreal, to the kitchen, where he finally let go of her hand and put a stool in front of her. "You can sit here."

She did as he asked and then watched him move around the immaculate kitchen. It might have been cleaner than her kitchen at home.

"Do you still eat anything?"

"Pretty much."

"Do you trust me?"

She knew he was talking about food but somehow his words held a deeper meaning. "I trust you."

He started to gather ingredients and as he did asked, "Tell me something about you that I don't know."

"Oh God, I'm not sure there is anything. I'm pretty boring."

"Why'd you become a therapist? You always wanted to be a pediatrician, if I remember correctly."

"I did but once I got into med school, I had a professor who was a therapist and I was blown away by some of the things I learned from her. And then when I found out I could help people with addictions, it was a no brainer."

"Do you like it?"

"I love it. I get to meet so many interesting people and also help them. Sure, I don't help everyone, but the ones I do help make up for it. What about you? I don't remember you ever wanting to cook?"

"It was one of those things that happened by accident. After I got clean, I went for a couple of years where I drank and ate badly. Then I realized that life wasn't for me. So I started working out and eating clean and that meant I had to cook. Soon I found out I was good at it and I even took classes to learn more."

"That's incredible." He was chopping vegetables and his hands were moving so fast. "Does that mean you don't drink?"

"Yeah, but not because of my addiction. Alcohol wasn't something I was addicted to and it never caused me to relapse. Mainly I don't drink because I don't want to. I figure I put my body through hell for several years so I have a lot to make up for."

"You look amazing." She realized what she'd said and felt her eyebrows raise.

He turned his head and looked at her. "Thanks. It's better than being all skin and bones."

"I more than liked how you looked back then but that's only because I didn't know this you existed."

His neck turned red and soon his whole face was the same hue. She'd embarrassed him.

That was unexpected.

And sexy.

"I kinda feel the same about you. You're – God how to say this without sounding like a perverted jackass – super stacked."

She laughed and for the first time in years felt completely relaxed with him. "You can thank my love of junk food and wine for that. Once I gave up trying to be model thin, I over-indulged and most of it went to my ass and boobs."

"You've got me rethinking what I'm about to feed you because anything that makes you look like that can't be all bad."

It was her turn to blush but she couldn't seem to look away from him. She'd fought with her body image for years when she was younger and it had taken her years of gaining weight to finally start loving her body.

The fact that he seemed to like it went a long way to telling her she had been right to stop obsessing.

"I –" She stumbled over her thoughts and paused. "I don't know what we're doing here." That was the best she could come up with.

"We're catching up and becoming friends again." He kept cooking and for a minute she let herself think that it was because he needed to keep his hands busy. But despite their kiss earlier, it seemed he only wanted to be friends.

"So we're going to be friends?"

"I hope so." He moved effortlessly around the kitchen.

Okay so he wanted to be friends. That was what she'd come there to find out and now she knew. She could be friends with him easily enough. Sure, that shouldn't be a problem. She could be friends with him and find a guy who wanted to date her. One who she liked. Maybe one who had a body like Wes. Oh and his hands. He needed to have expert hands like Wes's too.

"And more later."

Oh and he needed to be a nice guy. One who – wait did he just say something?

"What?"

"More. Friends first and then more."

He'd set the pan down that he was cooking with and was now facing her. Actually he'd moved closer to her and was now only a foot or so from where she sat.

She swallowed hard trying to understand what was happening. "You want...more?" she squeaked out.

"Lia, I don't know if we can have what we had before, or if it'll even turn into anything, but I do know that when I look at you, it's like those years apart just fade away. I refuse to spend more years fighting it."

She let out the breath she'd been holding. "Oh, God." She put a hand to her head. "Until this morning I thought you hated me and now you're standing in front of me offering me everything I've dreamed about for fourteen years. Am I dreaming? This is totally a dream. There's no way it can be real."

"You tell me." He stepped even closer, his hand reaching out to touch her face. His fingers were warm against her skin but somehow goosebumps popped up over her whole body. She wanted to look away, but his brown eyes were gleaming with heat and she wanted whatever he was about to offer, even if it was a dream.

"Please don't be a dream," she whispered right before his lips connected with hers. It was a chaste kiss, at least compared to the one earlier when she'd all but climbed his body, and it only lasted a few seconds. But when she pulled away, her whole body hummed with remembrance of a past she still longed for.

"Definitely not a dream."

Chapter 7

Wes was positive he should slow down to give Julia time to catch up with where he was. But one look, one touch, and he was back to being full-on in love with her.

Years had passed, anger had faded and what was left was love.

Pure and simple.

After their intense conversation and their kiss in the kitchen, he finished their food and they sat out at the bar to eat. He tried hard to keep topics light, asking about her friends and things they liked to do. He didn't want to push too far too fast.

"This is really amazing," she said as she took a bite of the stir fry he'd made them. "Who knew vegetables could be so good?"

"Thanks."

"You should put this on the menu. People would devour it."

"I might, but right now I have to keep it pretty simple. Otherwise I will be overwhelmed back there when we are busy."

"Well, feel free to make it for me anytime." She took another bite and then her eyes went big and she dropped her fork. "Oh my God, it's your night off and I'm sitting here taking up your time and making you cook."

He laughed. "I wanted to cook for you and," he shrugged, "this is where I would have been anyway. I like being here when it's quiet."

"There is something serene about it."

"I think I like it because it's mine. I've never owned anything this big before. Fuck, I've never even lived alone. I've always had a roommate and had to share space."

"I kinda know what you mean. A couple years before I moved back here, I bought myself a condo. I wanted something that was mine. The hospital was always swamped with people and I just rented the space for my office from them. But that condo...I loved it."

"You could do that here. Get a place of your own."

"I will eventually. Mom is fine and would be cool if I moved out now, but," she bit her bottom lip making him want to soothe it was his tongue, "I used up a lot of my savings when I moved my practice up here. I had to buy out my contract from the hospital down there and that took everything I had in savings plus what I made from the sale of my condo. I basically came home broke. Thankfully, I've had a year of no bills to help rectify that."

"Wow, I had no idea but I'm not far from being in the same boat. It took everything I had to get this place up and running. If not for Dax doing the labor for free, there is no way I would have been able to pull it off. It's one of the reasons I wanted to try and live with him as long as possible."

"I thought you were living with Joy?"

"Heard about that did ya?'" He smiled wondering what she'd thought when she'd found out. Had there been any jealousy? "I live with her now but only because walking in on my brother and Avery doing it on the kitchen counter is something I only need to live through once. Even once was too much."

"Are you kidding me?" She practically spit out her water.

"Believe me when I tell you I would never kid about something like that."

"Those two are like teenagers. Every time I turn around they are lip-locked."

"We were like that once," he said softly. Whenever they'd been together, they'd been touching. They'd been like magnets, coming together anytime they were near.

"And people hated it."

"They did." Their friends would groan and tell them to get a room almost daily. "We were pretty nauseating."

"We were young, what did we know?"

"How does that explain Dax and Avery or Brandon and Leah? Oh, and don't even get me started on Carly and Tony." The town was sex-crazed. Everywhere he went people were in love and making out.

It was starting to get to him.

Her laughter filled the empty room. "It is a little out of control. Last week I was walking through town and decided to stop in the gallery. As I browsed I came across Melanie and Logan tucked into a back corner making out."

"At least they were fully dressed. Or at least I hope they were. Anyway, that's why I moved out when I would have rather stayed to save some money."

"I like Joy. A lot actually. She's different from Avery, but also the same."

"We hit it off right away. I think it's something about us both being the outcasts of our family." He took another bite of his food and once he had swallowed said, "We're just friends."

"I know. She explained it to me when I found out and practically had a stroke."

"Were you...jealous?" He wasn't sure if her answer would make things easier or harder, but he needed to know.

"I was consumed with jealousy. It was beyond ridiculous."

Okay at least one part of him was hard at knowing she'd been jealous. And fuck if he didn't want to do something about it.

"Why is it so easy to talk to you?" she asked before he could speak again. "Even about things like this. Sex and jealousy."

"Probably because we know each other so well. You were my best friend and the one person I told everything to for four years. That comfort doesn't just disappear. You should know that."

"I do, but the therapist in me goes out the window when it comes to you. All bets are off and I can't make my mind or heart conform to what I think they should do."

Her honesty was like a punch to the gut. For all his worrying that he was pushing her or going too fast, it looked like he didn't have to worry. They seemed to be on the same page.

That page, however, was ripped and torn and somehow they were going to have to find a way to put it back together.

"The only day I have off is Monday and all my nights are spent here."

"All right," she said, kind of drawing it out.

He sighed. "What I'm trying to say, and obviously doing it badly, is that I'd like to see you again, maybe take you out, but I'm not sure when."

A bright smile lit up her face. "Well, I can set my own schedule and I have several days where I don't go in until later because I work into the evening."

"That helps, a little."

"What if I check my calendar and let you know." She was taking charge and that was new. She had always been tentative to make the plans and had no problem letting him guide the way. "Maybe we could have a breakfast date?"

"I'd like that." She slid her phone to him, he typed his info in, and then called himself so he would have her number. "There, now we are all set."

"I should probably get going." She scooted her bar stool back and hopped down. "I've taken up a lot of your time already."

Panicked that she would leave and he would never see her again he said, "Come in for a meal this week. Maybe tomorrow."

Her cheeks flushed and she looked down. "I'll let you know." She took a few steps toward the door but stopped and turned to face him. "Thanks for the meal and for, well, for being my friend again."

He couldn't make his mouth speak as she walked away. God what was wrong with him. Grabbing their plates he took them in back to clean up and practically threw them in the sink. Should he have kissed her? Man, did he want to kiss her. That first kiss was so spontaneous and unpredictable but it was everything. The feel of her lips under his and her hands on his body was what he dreamed about each night. It had been hard to stop but he'd known they'd needed to talk. And then, when he lightly kissed her in his kitchen, it was because he wanted the memory. Now every night when he was in there cooking, that would be what he thought of and imagined.

It was getting late, so after he cleaned up he headed for home. He found Joy on the couch eating pizza and watching TV.

"You're home late," she said around a mouthful of pizza.

"I had an unexpected guest."

"Oh yeah, who?"

"Julia." He knew now that Joy was aware that Julia was the woman he had dated back in the day. He wasn't sure why he hadn't told her before but something about telling people had felt odd to him.

"Julia as in your ex, Julia who, by the way, you never told me was your ex? I only found out because I opened my big mouth and mentioned living with you. You should have seen her face. I thought she was going to faint right there on Leah and Brandon's deck."

"She told me about that." He smiled remembering the story and how she was so relaxed as she did. "And I never told you because...well I don't know why. I just wanted to keep her name out of it."

"If it matters, I like her. A lot actually. She's nice and real and well, if I liked women she'd totally be my type with just her body alone."

He gaped at her.

"What, she's hot in a buttoned-up, executive type of way. But you just know that naked she is rocking those curves. Was she always stacked?"

He shook his head and sat down next to her, shoving her feet off the couch. "No, the curves are new."

"But you like them right?"

He choked out a cough. How was it that she always got him to talk about shit like this. "Yeah I like them, okay. Who wouldn't?"

She pointed her pizza at him. "So what's the deal with her coming by? As far as I was aware you and she weren't on speaking terms."

"We weren't until Saturday night." He sunk deeper into the couch. "She showed up to Dockside on a date."

"Shut the front door!"

"It's a long story but I wouldn't have known she was there except that her date wanted to thank the chef."

"What a douche."

"As much as I want to agree with that, it also feels good that people are liking the food."

"Yeah, yeah, yeah, you're amazing and all that shit, but what happened then?"

"When I saw her I hesitated as you'd expect, but then I pulled it together enough to speak. She didn't say a word, only her date. It was quick and then I was back in the kitchen wondering what the hell had just happened."

"None of that explains why you were with her tonight?" She straightened her leg and kicked him.

"I'm getting there." He once again shoved her foot off the couch. "After I closed, I went to leave and there she was, sitting outside against the building waiting for me."

"Classic romance movie move."

He rolled his eyes. "We talked, but I was so dumbfounded that I hadn't really wrapped my mind around things yet."

"By things do you mean that you still love her?"

He stared at her like she had two heads. How had she come to that conclusion?

"It's pretty obvious, at least to me. But don't worry, I won't tell anyone."

He pushed that from his mind and went on with his story. "After that night, I spent all day Sunday thinking about what I wanted, and then this morning, I went by her work and waited for her. She was surprised to see me the same as I was seeing her on Saturday night, but she invited me in and we talked. We came to the conclusion that we needed to be friends. But then I went and did something crazy right before I left. I told her I was sick of missing her and didn't want to do it anymore."

Joy's eyes went wide. "I would have never pegged you for a sap."

He threw a pillow at her. "Shut up."

"Let me guess, she showed up at Dockside tonight wondering what you meant by it?"

"How'd you guess?"

"Because it's seriously a RomCom movie line. It's so exact that I feel like I should write the screenplay and send it to Hollywood."

"You know what, since you already know how it ends, I don't need to tell you." He crossed his arms and waited.

"Fine," she huffed out and threw up her arms. "I won't say another word." She mimicked zipping her lips.

He gave in and kept going. "She immediately went into this whole thing with her dad and us, that part doesn't matter though, but when she finished there was all this heat in the room and somehow...we kissed."

Joy's eyes went wide but as promised she didn't say a word.

"After that, things became easy, just like they used to be. I cooked her dinner, we ate, and the whole time we talked. It was all so natural."

Joy raised her hand like she was in school.

"What?"

"Did you kiss anymore?"

Leave it to her to cue in on that one thing. "Just once, but nothing like the first one."

She raised her hand again.

"Just talk."

"How did you leave it?"

"We are going to be friends as we maybe work our way to something more."

"Wow," she said. "You guys moved fast."

"Why should I go slow when I know what I want?"

"And what you want is Julia?"

"She's what I've always wanted."

"See, you love her." Her smile was evil and knowing.

"Have I mentioned how much I hate you recently?"

"You'd be bored without me." She sat forward and took another slice of pizza. "We missed you at Leah and Brandon's on Saturday."

He'd wished he'd been able to go and enjoy the summer and fun with all his friends. But it just hadn't been possible with the hours he put in at the restaurant. "Was it fun?"

"Surprisingly, yeah. There were a lot of people there I didn't know, but I got to meet a few and they seemed nice."

"Any single men for you?" He knew she was on a dating sabbatical as she called it, but he also knew she was lonely.

"Ugh, no. And why is it that everyone wants me to find a man? I don't need a man. Men suck. Present company excluded."

"I just don't want you to avoid trying something new just because you're afraid."

"I'm not afraid of dating." She closed her eyes and dropped her head to her chest.

"If you say you are good, then I won't bother you about it anymore." He started to stand but her foot came up and pushed him back down.

"Let's say I was afraid. How would I get over that?"

"I can't say for sure but usually facing your fear helps."

"This isn't like falling off a horse. This is me being afraid that I'll fall right back into old habits and sleep with guys on first dates."

He sat quietly because he had no idea what to say to her. And then a thought popped into his head. "Why don't you talk to Julia? She could probably help you."

"Therapy. You think I should go to therapy?"

"No, I think you should talk to your friend who happens to be a therapist. I don't know for sure, but if I had to guess, she's probably pretty good at what she does."

She pursed her lips. "Maybe. I'll think about it."

"Think fast because I hate seeing you unhappy."

She flipped him off as he stood up. Shaking his head he walked down the short hallway to his room. After shedding his clothes, and pulling on sweats, he quickly hit the bathroom before falling down onto his bed.

He was tired after two sleepless nights, and now that he and Julia had talked, when he closed his eyes, he knew that he'd actually be able to fall asleep.

The best part was that he had that kiss to relive as he did so.

This might be his best night of sleep in fourteen years.

Chapter 8

Staring at the ceiling fan in her childhood bedroom, Julia was shocked she wasn't already asleep. The last three days had been the hardest of her life and it was a life that included losing Wes and her dad dying.

Malcolm, one of her drug rehab patients had overdosed.

He'd been clean for over two years when she'd first started seeing him six months ago. And now he was dead.

She couldn't help but link the two events.

Was it her fault? Had she not done enough to keep him clean? Had something she'd said or done made him start using again?

It was all too crushing.

Turning to her side, she began to once again, for probably the three hundredth time, go over everything she'd ever said to him during group or in one-on-one sessions. Nothing came to mind that would be a trigger, at least as far as she could remember.

But that meant nothing.

Now her focus needed to be on the other patients in her group rehab who had been friends with Malcolm. That was why she was so tired. She'd offered her services basically twenty-four hours a day for anyone who needed to talk.

And boy had they.

She'd been in her office for three days straight, and then at night when she finally did come home, a few had called, needing to talk. Tonight had been no different. Cassie, a young woman who was only eighteen, was having a hard time because she and Malcolm had been close. Not girlfriend/boyfriend close, but sister/brother close. She'd spent an hour on the phone with her before finally hanging up.

She heard a ding and groaned when she saw her phone light up. She wanted to help, but damn she needed sleep.

Picking up her phone, she blinked twice when she saw who it was. Wes.

Her heart started beating rapidly in her chest.

She hadn't thought about him in three days because her life had been so crazy, but just seeing his name on the screen brought it all back.

Wes:

Are you alive?

It was a weirdly worded question and she wondered for a minute if Avery had told him what was going on.

Julia:

Uh yeah

Wes:

That's good to know.

She waited for more but nothing came. One minute passed, then two and finally five. Why had he texted only to ask her that and nothing else? Not willing to let it go, she texted him.

Julia:

Is something up?

Wes:

No...Maybe. I thought you would have called by now.

Julia:

Oh. You know you could have contacted me?

Wes:

I guess I could have.

I hate this. Come down.

What? Had he just asked her to come down? Was he there? Jumping out of bed, she ran to her window, pulled open the shade and looked down. Sure enough there he was.

What was he doing there? She heard her phone ding again in her hand.

Wes:

Please

That one word from him was all it took to melt her. She was so spent emotionally that she wasn't capable of stopping herself from needing to be with him.

Quietly, so her mom wouldn't hear her, she tiptoed downstairs and out the front door. He was leaning against the hood of his truck, legs and arms crossed.

Everything heavy inside her evaporated and, instead of doing the safe thing and holding back, she ran toward him. He caught her and wrapped her up in his arms as the tears that she'd held in for days finally fell.

"Lia, honey, what's wrong?" His hand stroked up and down her back.

She wasn't able to answer through her tears so instead she just shook her head back and forth against his chest and kept on crying. When the tears finally ran dry, she lifted her head and looked up at him.

"I'm sorry." She wiped her eyes with one of her hands.

Smiling down at her he lifted his hands to her face and wiped away the remainder of her tears with his thumbs. "I hate to complain because I got to hold you in my arms, but I'd love to know what's wrong?"

She stepped back from him, took his hand in hers and walked them both to the porch. "It's been a really bad week."

"If you don't want to talk about it, I understand." They sat on one of the steps, him not letting go of her hand.

"I think I'd like to actually."

He squeezed her hand in a reassuring gesture.

"On Monday night, one of my rehab patients overdosed."

"Oh no." His voice was low and the concern was real.

"His name was Malcolm and he'd been with me for about six months. But before he came to my group, he had been clean for two years." She shook her head side-to-side. "Two years clean, and then six months with me, and he goes back to using and dies." She looked up at him through her tear-filled eyes. "Is this my fault? Did I cause this?"

"God no," he said. "Why would you think that?"

"Because it's the only thing that makes sense."

"You are smarter than that. You know that if someone wants to use, it's on them, not on anyone else."

"I thought I knew that, but Malcolm was doing so well, I just can't figure out what went wrong."

"You'll work through it and figure it out. I'm sure of it."

"I'm glad someone has faith in me." She weakly smiled up at him.

"Let me ask you something, what have you been doing since you found out about Malcolm?"

"I've worked non-stop and made myself available to any of my group patients in case they needed me."

"And have they?"

"I mean, yeah. I've been so busy that I haven't been getting home until after nine, and even then, they call me at all hours of the night."

"Do those seem like people who have lost faith in you?"

She looked down at her bare feet. "I guess I never looked at it like that."

"Hey," he used his free hand to lift her chin back up, "don't doubt yourself. Those people need you. Right now you might be the only thing stopping one of them from doing what Malcolm did."

"When did you get so smart?"

"It took a while but somewhere along the way it happened."

"You came to see me." It was more of a statement than a question.

"When I didn't hear from you, I just kept thinking I had pushed too hard, too fast, and I needed to see you."

"You didn't push too hard, too fast. In fact, I kinda wish it was faster."

He looked down at her and lowered his forehead to hers. "You can't say things like that to me tonight."

"Why not?" Her eyes searched his.

"Because tonight you need a friend, someone to lean on. Not someone who desperately wants to get you naked."

Her breath hitched at his words. "You want to get me naked?"

His chocolate brown eyes turned dark. "So, so much."

"How do you know that's not what I need?"

Lightly, he kissed her lips and then pulled back. "Because I know you, and I refuse to have you regret our first time."

She raised her eyebrows. "If I remember correctly, I did regret our first time."

Their first time had been in the middle of their junior year. They'd been going out for over a year, and because of that, they thought they'd been ready. Turns out they weren't. It wasn't everything it was cracked up to be, and when it ended, she cried and cried because she thought she'd done something wrong. The whole thing had taken less than three minutes and she'd been in pain the whole time. He'd assured her that she'd done nothing wrong and now that she was older she knew that. But at the time, she regretted ever making the decision to have sex.

"Even more of a reason for you not to regret this second, first time."

"So sure of yourself that there will be a second, first time?"

"I'm not sure of anything where you are concerned, Lia. Somehow, after all these years, we have found our way back to each other. I have to hope that means something. That someday soon, you and I will have our second, first time."

They were still close, his hand still holding her face. "I have a feeling our second first time is going to be out of this world."

He held her gaze for seconds with only the sounds of the night around them. "I should go." Yet he didn't move.

She licked her lips and his eyes darted down to her mouth. More seconds ticked by. Somehow they seemed to get even closer until his lips were mere centimeters from hers. "Or," she said, it coming out breathless.

"One kiss," he said, his warm breath hitting her lips just before his lips did.

Her mouth opened under his as he began his slow assault on her. Gentle, tender and loving was how she would later describe the kiss. He never pressed, never pressured. It was a kiss of seduction. One that was meant to make her toes curl, and it succeeded. When he pulled back, he kept his face close.

"Think of me tonight."

She couldn't speak, but she gave him a small nod. She sat, her ass glued to the step, while he stood and walked to his truck. Minutes after his taillights had disappeared into the night sky, she still sat in the same spot.

Her lips tingled from their kiss and her head was a jumbled mess, but her heart knew, without a doubt, what it wanted.

Wes.

It had always wanted Wes. Even on that night so many years ago, when they'd fumbled in the dark making love for the first time, he was what she'd wanted.

Sighing into the night, she stood up and walked back into her house. Not many people got a chance to have a second, first time. She was going to do her best not to fuck it up.

Normally on Fridays, she worked most of the day, but not that Friday. It was the day of Malcolm's funeral so she had canceled all her appointments. When she arrived at the funeral home, she shakily got out of her car. She took a steadying breath before she started walking toward the building. She was steps from the door when she felt a hand at her back. Turning she found Wes walking beside her.

"What are you doing here?"

"You shouldn't have to do this alone."

He was cleaned up, wearing a black suit with a gray shirt and black tie. He'd shaved and his smooth face looked younger somehow.

"But what about the restaurant?" It was noon and she knew that Dockside was open on Fridays at eleven.

"We have a limited menu until dinner and Sabrina is handling it. Everyone will understand."

Biting her bottom lip, she stood on her toes and kissed his cheek. "Thank you."

It meant the world to her that he'd somehow known how hard this would be for her and took time out of his busy day to be there. They walked into the building and found it jam-packed. As she looked around, she saw most of the people who were in group with Malcolm and several of the other group therapists. She also saw Malcolm's mom and dad who she'd met only once. Malcolm had been twenty, which meant he wasn't a minor and there had been no need to meet with family. He'd come to group meetings voluntarily, not because he was in rehab.

Wes stayed close and walked with her as she gave her condolences to the family. When they approached her group patients, she greeted them all and introduced Wes.

"Doc J is this your boyfriend?" one of the younger members, Chris, asked.

She turned and looked up at Wes. "Just a friend," she said.

"And someone who knows what this is all about." She was shocked he'd said that.

"No way, you were an addict?" Carrie asked.

"I was. For a lot of years."

"Did Doc J help you?"

He looked at her before answering. "You could say that but really I got clean because I wanted to. And just like you guys, I had a terrific therapist who helped me navigate the whole process."

She was pulled away by one of her colleagues but Wes stayed and continued to talk to the group members. Most of them were younger, teens or early twenties, but she did have two in their thirties.

When the service started, Wes found her, and together they sat, holding hands the whole time. When it ended, they walked out like they'd walked in, hand-in-hand.

"You doing okay?"

She shrugged. "Not really, but this is life, isn't it?"

He squeezed her hand. "Those kids in there, they love you. The way they talk about you and what you do for them...it's impressive."

"I don't do that much."

"That's not what they told me. They said that you gave them your personal phone number and that they can call whenever. Not only that, but if they miss a meeting, you come to their homes to check on them. Julia, there isn't another therapist in the world who would do that."

"I just...I want them to succeed. I want them to have the lives they deserve and not to always be labeled as a druggie or an addict. There is more to them than that."

"I hope it's okay, but after talking to them, I realized that a couple of them need jobs, and well, I need people, so I offered them jobs."

She stopped walking and turned to stare at him. "You offered them jobs?"

"Uh yeah." He hung his head. "Is that not okay?"

Her mouth was dry and her brain wasn't functioning. He'd done something for others without even thinking of himself.

Words failed her so instead she threw herself into his arms. He caught her and gripped her tightly, whispering in her ear, "I guess it's okay."

She nodded against his chest, holding on for dear life. When she felt like she could speak again, she loosened her grip, just a little, and looked up at him.

"I don't deserve your friendship, let alone more. I was so horrible to you."

"Fuck that, Julia. You didn't do anything that anyone else wouldn't have done when faced with the same situation. If you want to talk about being deserving, well I think I get to decide what I deserve, and I think that's you. So deal with it."

His words weren't angry, only firm. "It is your life."

"Damn right it is. And I'm sick of living it without you."

She wanted to be brave and bold like him and take what she wanted. But could she? Licking her lips, she leaned a little more into him and said against his lips, "Come home with me," and then kissed his lips.

"I thought you'd never ask," he said after a second.

She smiled as he began pulling her toward his truck. "We'll come back to pick-up your car later."

"Wait." She stopped walking and dropped her head backward. "It's the middle of the day and my mom is there. Night is one thing, but I can't bring you home for sex in the middle of the afternoon."

"It's a good thing that my place is empty then." He grinned and winked.

"Let's go." This time it was her pulling him, even though she had no idea where he was parked.

Once they finally got to his truck, he opened the door for her, but before she could climb in, he spun her so she was facing him. "Be sure, Lia." His voice was low and deep, running chills over her whole body.

Gripping his tie in her fist, she pulled him even closer. "Get in the truck, Wes, unless you want all these people to see us fuck."

His breathing hitched and his eyes bore into hers with a heat she never could have imagined. "Damn I like this new you."

He gave her a quick kiss before turning her around and practically shoving her into his truck. She laughed as she fastened her seatbelt waiting for him to get in. When the door opened and he jumped in, she let out a giggle and then slapped her hand over her mouth.

"What was that?" he said, starting the truck and backing out.

"This is all so comical to me. We were at a fucking funeral and now we are beelining to go have sex. Second, first-time sex at that." She shook her head, laughing again. "My life is one big random set of events."

"We don't have to do this," he said.

She dipped her chin and rolled her eyes. "We're absolutely doing this. This is the one thing that I for sure know I want. Everything else...I have no clue."

He gripped her hand across the seat and gave it a squeeze. It didn't take long to get to his place, and once parked, they both jumped out. He came around and took her hand as they walked up to his apartment.

"I didn't think to ask, is Joy here?"

"She shouldn't be, but honestly I never know her schedule." They reached the door. "If she is, I'll tell her to leave and she will understand."

He put the key in the lock and turned the knob. "We can't kick her out."

"It's either she goes and we have sex, or she stays and we have sex, and I promise you, this will not be sweet eighteen-year-old sex." He opened the door and ushered her in, closing it behind them. From behind, his lips came down on her neck and bit. "This is going to be loud and dirty."

She shivered and felt him even when he pulled away. "Joy!" he shouted.

The apartment stayed silent.

"Looks like we're all alone."

He was still behind her and when she turned to face him, he was pulling off his jacket and tie. She joined in and kicked off her shoes. He closed the distance between them, wrapping one arm around her body and tugging her to him so she was tightly pressed up against his chest.

Lowering his mouth, she assumed he was going to kiss her, but instead, he took her bottom lip between his teeth and pulled, his eyes never leaving hers. It was possibly the most erotic thing that had ever happened to her.

She was about to change that.

Gripping his hair in her fists, she held him to her and slipped her tongue out to lick his bottom lip. That was apparently enough for both of them. Their mouths came together in a passionate kiss. It was beyond out of control. She couldn't get enough and wanted to eat him alive. His hands were roaming her body and when his fingers lifted her shirt and grazed her bare skin, she whimpered into his mouth.

He must have understood, because from there things got even more out of control. Clothes began coming off and were thrown all around. Kisses on lips turned to kisses over faces and shoulders and chests. She wasn't sure how they ended up in his room, but the next thing she knew they were horizontal on a bed and his hand was trailing up her leg to where she was warm, wet and ready.

Her body was on fire and while she was a fan of foreplay, this was not the day for it. Today there was only one thing she wanted.

Flipping him to his back, she moved on top of him. His chest was muscled and toned begging her to kiss it. So she did. "Condom?" she said against his skin.

"Drawer," he choked out when she licked his nipple.

She reached over, opened the drawer and found the brand new box. Opening the box was difficult though while Wes's mouth was doing wicked things to her breasts.

"I can't believe these are the same tits," he said against her skin. She squeaked when he bit one nipple and had to brace herself from falling over on top of him. Giving up on opening the box normally, she tore at it until condoms fell out everywhere. Picking one up, she tore it open with her teeth. Scooting back out of his reach, she bit her lip when she saw his cock.

"Is it bigger?"

He growled, actually growled. "Put the goddamn condom on, Lia."

She slid it down slowly, torturing him with each second it took. When it was all the way on, she lifted her leg and moved back over the top of him.

Smiling, she leaned forward to kiss him again. He was throbbing against her pussy and, because she couldn't wait any longer, she slid him inside her.

"Holy shit," he huffed out and the look on his face was pure bliss.

They started moving together in unison and this was one thing that was exactly the same as before. They knew each other and knew how their bodies moved. It was like riding a bike.

A bike that was made just for you.

A bike that fits you perfectly.

She loved this fucking bike.

In minutes, he flipped them over so he was on top. "My turn to be in charge now." He kissed her as he leveled himself up over her and began to pound into her. Her fingers were digging into his forearms where he was holding himself up and her eyes were looking between them where they were coming together.

It was something she never thought to do when they were younger, but now she needed to see it. Needed to know what they looked like.

"Fuck" he swore above her making her eyes flicker back to his. "Please tell me you're close."

She couldn't speak, was too close to answer so instead she arched her back off the bed, pushing her pelvis closer to him. Her hands reached over her head so she could gain even more traction to push against him. That was all she needed and soon her whole body was shaking with her orgasm. Wes obviously felt her go over because his face tensed and he pushed himself deep inside her one last time, holding himself still over top of her.

The one thing that hadn't changed in fourteen years, was how it felt to have him pulsing inside her.

Chapter 9

He tried to slow his breathing but it was almost impossible. He'd just had the orgasm to end all orgasms and his body was already wanting to do it again. Trying not to think about how good it felt to be inside her, he opened his eyes to find Julia staring up at him.

She was so gorgeous with her hair scattered all over his pillow and her face flushed from their lovemaking.

"I hate to be cliche after sex, but you are beautiful."

A lazy smile appeared on her face. "I'll let it slide just this once."

He bent to kiss her tenderly and then rolled off, quickly disposing of the condom. She turned sideways and curled into his side.

"I guess what they say about things getting better with age is true."

He turned his head and examined her. "Yeah, I'm pretty sure if it had been like this years ago, I would have followed you to Tennessee."

She laughed but it didn't reach her eyes.

"Is it too soon to joke about?" He smiled hoping to lighten the mood.

"Maybe." She stifled a yawn. "I'm still working through what I did to you."

Turning his whole body, he used his finger to push a piece of hair off her face. "Take the time you need but know that I am over it. When I look at my life today, I'm happy with how it has turned out. Sure there were some bad years, but I wouldn't have the good without the bad."

"God, I want to be as good as the therapist you had." Now her smile was real.

"He was good, but listening to those kids talk about you today, I have no doubt you are already at least as good."

Her lips touched his in a sweet kiss. "You know how to make a girl feel good."

"As much as I'd like to stay here and make you feel good several more times. I really should get to the restaurant."

She sat up in a hurry. "Oh my God, yes, you need to go."

"Finished with me already?"

"Hell no, but I don't want to be the reason you miss work."

Sitting up, he kissed her one more time. "I would gladly miss work for you if I had anybody else there who could cook." He stood up and began looking for clean clothes to wear for work. "I need to take a quick shower. Take your time getting dressed." He gave her one last glance, her breasts barely covered by the sheet. Shaking his head, he hurried out of the room and across the hall to the only bathroom in the apartment.

Once he was showered and dressed, he found Julia in the living room, picking up his clothes that he'd discarded.

"You didn't have to do that."

"I don't mind." She sat and slipped on each one of her shoes.

His mind was going at full speed at how easy this was for her. Nothing about it felt easy to him. He was already in so deep.

Before he could stop himself, he said, "This isn't a one-time thing for me."

She looked up from the couch blinking several times. "It isn't for me either."

"Okay, I just needed to say that. I don't know what happens next but I'd like to keep seeing you." He was too old to play games and even though this was complicated, he had to be honest.

"You're off on Monday's right? What if we plan a date? I can be off too and we can have the whole day together."

"We can do that." He took her hand and pulled her up so she was standing in front of him. "You could also come to the restaurant tonight and have dinner."

She tilted her head and squinted. "Would that be okay? I wanted to do that but I wasn't sure what you would think."

"I would love it." He liked knowing she was also a little insecure about them.

"So we're telling people? About us?"

"I wasn't planning on hiding it, if that's what you mean."

"I just didn't know where we stood on that."

And then it hit him. Maybe she didn't want people to know. "Do you not want to tell people?"

She grabbed his arm. "No, I mean yes." She took a deep breath. "I am all right with people knowing I just don't know what to say. Are we sleeping together or are we more or maybe we're just friends."

He leaned down so their faces were close together. "Not that I care what other people think, but what if we tell the truth? We are dating and seeing what this is."

She nodded. "You're so calm and I'm a total disaster."

"I don't see a disaster. I see a woman who is strong and confident. A woman who knows what she wants and goes after it. A woman who, with just a touch, has me hotter than I've been in my whole life."

"Wow. I kinda want to be that woman who you see."

"You are. You just aren't looking in the right places." His lips feathered over hers. "Now, I really do have to go."

She pushed at his chest. "Yes, let's go." She followed him to the door. "I'll come by later for dinner."

They walked out the door and down to his truck. He dropped her back at the funeral home where she'd left her car and then headed to Dockside. The place wasn't busy, just a few people enjoying a late meal.

He found Sabrina at the bar. "How'd it go?"

"Easy."

"Anything I need to know about?"

"Nope."

"Ya know, Sabrina, I used to like that you didn't talk my ear off, but now it's starting to drive me crazy."

"You asked me questions and I answered. Why do I need to give a long explanation when there isn't a need for one?"

He shook his head and went around the bar. Pouring himself a glass of water, he took a long drink before setting it down on the bar. "True, but I want this place to be like a family, and when you barely talk to me, that makes it hard."

"Think of me like a hormonal teenager who hates her parents and locks herself in her room."

He inclined his head to her. "At least I know you have a sense of humor."

"Why are you so chatty all of a sudden anyway? Does it have something to do with why you weren't here today?"

"No." Hmmm, maybe it did. Was he chatty? Could that be because he was happy?

"You're a horrible liar."

"If you must know, I was at a funeral." That wasn't the whole story, but she didn't need to know that."

Her face fell. "Oh, I'm sorry."

"It's fine. It wasn't someone I knew. I just went as support for a friend."

"Well I didn't mind filling in. I can't claim to be a good cook, but I can do burgers and fries and follow directions."

"I appreciate that. I'm going to have to look into finding someone to help me out in the kitchen. If we stay this busy, there's no way I can keep up the schedule of being here six days a week for twelve hours."

"I might know someone."

"How the hell do you know all these people?" First, it was the baker, Dani, and now she knew a cook.

"I just know a lot of people. When you're a bartender, people talk."

"You were right on with Dani so set it up and I'll meet him or her."

"It's a him and I'll have him try and stop by this weekend."

He nodded and headed in back to get things ready for the dinner rush. Sabrina had done a good job of cleaning up and she'd even peeled more potatoes. He got busy making jambalaya and mac and cheese so it would be ready for the dinner customers. Cooking was like second nature to him and that meant his mind wandered back to earlier in the day.

Sex with Julia had blown his mind. When they'd been teenagers, they hadn't known any better and it was quick and easy. While they'd loved each other, it was nothing like what they'd done today. Today there had been so much emotion and power in their lovemaking, it was overwhelming.

He'd wanted nothing more than to stay and keep loving her, but he had responsibilities that couldn't be pushed aside.

When his evening wait staff started coming in, he glanced at the clock and saw it was already four. That meant they would get busy at any minute. He wondered what time Julia would stop by. Would she come alone or would she come with friends?

Not that it mattered, but he hoped she came when it wasn't packed so he could scoot her off to an empty corner and kiss her.

Orders started coming in making him busy for what seemed like hours. When he started to slow down, he noticed it was after eight.

Had she forgotten? Was she not coming?

He was plating a burger and fries when Sabrina stuck her head through the swinging door.

"Your brother and Avery are here if you have a minute."

"Yeah, this is the last order for now."

"There's someone else with them too."

Could it be Julia? Had she come with Dax and Avery?

Throwing off his apron and hairnet, he pushed the door open to walk out into the restaurant. The place was still busy, with lots of people at the bar and out on the deck. He scouted the room looking for Dax when he felt a hand on his arm.

"Hey," the voice he'd been hearing in his head for hours said.

He swung his head around so fast that he got dizzy. She looked good enough to eat and he'd skipped lunch and dinner.

"What took you so long?" He gripped her waist, pulling her to him.

"I thought I'd have a better chance of seeing you if I waited until later in the night."

"Smartest woman ever." He leaned down and touched his lips to hers.

"This is a new turn of events," he heard his brother's voice from behind him.

"If you want to live, you'll go away," he said grinning down at Julia.

"No can do, bucko. Avery wants to eat and that means you need to get your ass back in the kitchen."

He groaned and stepped back from Julia. He found Dax and Avery both looking at him with amused faces.

"Hey, Wes," Avery singsonged, "how's it going?"

He looked back at Julia. "Have I mentioned how much I hate my family?"

"He's just pissed because he has to work and can't get you naked," Avery said.

"You were so sweet and nice when I first met you. What the hell happened?"

Dax put his arm around her. "I corrupted her."

During all the back and forth, Julia never spoke and instead watched with humor in her eyes. "Come on, let's go find a table." He took her hand and walked through the crowd of people until he found an empty table. He sat down next to her with Dax and Avery sitting across from them.

"You guys want to pick from the menu or you want me to just pick for you?"

"I want the mac and cheese and some grilled chicken," Avery said.

Dax shrugged. "I'll eat anything."

He looked at Julia. "Anything works for me."

He nodded. "Good I'll go back in a few and get it going." He squeezed her hand under the table. "How was your week?" he asked Dax and Avery.

"Oh no. No, no, no," Avery said. "Don't even try to get out of telling me what the hell is going on. All I know is that Julia called and asked to have a late dinner here. Here. A place that only days ago, she would have never stepped foot in." She glared at him. "Speak now."

He looked at his brother for help.

Lifting his hands in surrender Dax said, "Don't look at me. I have no control over her," to which Avery elbowed him in the side.

He shook his head, chuckling. "Julia and I have come to a truce." He glanced sideways at her. "More than that really. We are friends."

"Friends is one thing, but the way you grabbed her a few minutes ago is not something friends do. I have never walked into Julia's house and grabbed her around the waist, all the while lowering my face closer to hers and then kissing her."

"For the record," Dax spoke up, "I would be completely on board if you wanted to do that."

That earned him a glare from Avery, but both he and Julia laughed.

"Why is it that when it comes to girl on girl action, men all of a sudden don't care if you kiss someone else," Julia said?

"Hey," he said, "I didn't say a thing. That was all Dax."

"So you're saying you don't want Avery and me to kiss?"

He leaned down so his face was right on top of hers. "Is it too soon to say I don't want you kissing anyone else?" His voice was low but he was sure Avery and Dax could hear him.

Her smile was electric. "Not too soon and perfect answer by the way.

"Okay, now I know you two are more than friends."

Wes laughed and stood. "Julia will fill you in while I go make your food." He took a couple of steps before quickly turning back and striding back to Julia. Taking her hand, he pulled her up and into his body and took her mouth in a searing kiss. She immediately melted into him, giving him complete access to her mouth. He ended it before it was too late to end it and gave her a quick smile before leaving.

As he walked away he heard Avery say, "Dax why don't you ever kiss me like that?"

Chapter 10

Julia didn't trust herself to sit without reaching back and grabbing her chair. The man fried her brains. He made her a complete idiot.

She loved it.

"I can see by the goofy smile that you are already in deep." Avery was giving her a smug look.

"Can I plead the fifth?"

"No you can't." She turned to Dax. "I love you but I need you to leave this table."

Rolling his eyes, Dax gave Avery a kiss on her head as he stood. "Try not to make the interrogation too tough."

"You really lucked out with Dax. He is one of the good guys."

"Don't even try to weasel your way out of this. Talk."

"What do you want me to say, Avery, that somehow, someway he forgives me? That when I showed up here on Monday night to talk to him, we ended up kissing. What about him showing up at the funeral this morning because he knew I would be having a hard time? Do you need to know all of that?"

She wasn't loud or angry, but she needed to make her point.

"Can we start with the kiss and come back to everything else?" Avery tapped her index finger to her lip.

A laugh bubbled up and out of her, and soon Avery was laughing with her. "This is so insane." She covered her face with her hands.

"Why is it insane? You still like him and he, obviously, still likes you."

"Because it's been years, and what, we're both just not over the other person? That's fiction, stuff like that just doesn't happen."

"Except that things like that do happen. Look at Addison and Ryan. He moved here after meeting her twice. Love doesn't work on a timeline."

"I didn't say I was in love with him." She was, but she wasn't ready for Avery to know that yet.

Avery again gave her an *are you kidding me* look. "Moving on, tell me about the kiss."

She surprised herself by saying, "Wouldn't you rather hear about the sex?"

Avery's eyes went wide and she shouted, "What!"

Julia sat back and smiled. She loved it when her friend got all riled up.

"You slept together? When? Where? Holy shit, I have so many questions."

"Calm down," she shook her head chuckling, "and I'll tell you."

"I'm calm."

Where to start. "When I got here Monday, we talked and decided to be friends and also to maybe see each other. I promised to call him, but when Malcolm died, that all went out the window. I was working twenty-hour days and barely sleeping, so thinking about Wes went on the back burner. But on Thursday night he showed up at my house wondering why I hadn't called or come by. He was like a life preserver when I was drowning. I cried on him for who knows how long and he just let me as he held me. Then we talked, which was hard, because all I really wanted to do was take him inside and throw him on my bed. But I didn't because it wasn't right and I was an emotional mess. Then today, as I'm walking into the funeral, there he is. Dressed in a suit no less."

Avery's hand was over her heart. "He came to the funeral to support you."

She understood the look on Avery's face. She had been there and it was still the most romantic thing that she'd ever heard. "It was so Wes. He is always thinking of other people."

"Please tell me you didn't do it at the funeral? I mean if you did, I still want to hear about it, but I might lose a little respect for you." She paused. "No, you know what, I might have more respect for you."

"We didn't do it at the funeral. We went back to his place."

Her face fell. "That's not nearly as cool but I still want to hear about it."

"Thanks," she said sarcastically.

"So you went back to his place?"

"And that was it."

"That was it? Details girl. I need details."

"I don't know what you want?" She'd had friends before but never friends who she talked about her sexual experiences with. This was new.

"How was it?"

"Life changing." She smiled and closed her eyes remembering the feel of him inside her. "It was so much better than it had been all those years ago. It was like we were one person instead of two."

"Wow, that sounds incredible."

"It was."

"So what's this mean? Are you guys together?"

Wasn't that the million-dollar question. "We're dating."

Avery pursed her lips and nodded slowly. "Okay, that makes sense except...you guys already know everything about each other and that's the only reason people date."

"Why are you trying to ruin this for me?" She didn't want to rush this, did she?

"I'm not, really. I just don't want either of you to get hurt."

"I'm going into this with my eyes completely wide open. Am I afraid this won't last? Yes, sure I am because nothing is guaranteed in this world. I, of all people, know that better than anyone. But this is Wes, the love of my life, and if my choices are having him for just a bit or not having him at all, I am going to take every minute I can to be with him."

Avery was smiling at her oddly when she finished speaking. "Well, I for one, am rooting for this to work out. Happy endings are the best."

"I take it things with Dax are amazing as always?"

"He's the best even though he does work like a million hours."

"It won't always be that way."

"I know, I just miss him when he's gone." She twirled her hair in her finger. "Is it bad that I'm annoyed that he hasn't proposed yet? I know we've only been together three months, but we talk about marriage all the time and have basically planned our elopement. Why won't he propose?"

The therapist in her came out. "Why are you in such a hurry?"

"I'm not, I just want to be married. Being single was the worst time of my life, but these last three months with Dax have been amazing. I want to know that it's always going to be like that."

Before she could open her mouth to say anything, Dax and Wes were standing there.

"It is going to be like this forever. Nothing is going to change that." He knelt next to her chair, digging into his pocket and coming out with a jewelry box. "And the only reason I haven't asked you before now is that I didn't want to rush you." He opened the box revealing a gorgeous princess cut diamond. "I bought this ring right after you moved in with me for good. I knew the minute I saw you that you were it for me. Marry me, Avery, be my wife, my everything."

Avery was crying but she nodded and whispered, "Yes," before throwing herself into Dax's arms. Julia looked over to Wes and smiled as he also watched what was happening. When he caught her eyes, she grinned even wider.

"Oh my God, I'm engaged!" Avery shouted.

Julia stood up and went over to hug both her and Dax. "Congrats guys. This is so exciting."

Wes did the same and then stood next to her, taking her hand. Avery and Dax were caught up in each other so they weren't paying any attention to them.

"That was a surprise, huh," she said.

"Not really. I went with him to buy the ring."

"You knew?" She looked up at him.

"Yep." He winked at her and then pulled her in closer to him. "Come with me."

It wasn't a question, and she knew without a doubt, what they were going to do when they were alone. She followed him into the kitchen where they were alone. But he kept pulling her until they were in some kind of storage closet. As soon as the door closed, he had her pushed up against it.

"Fuck I missed you." His mouth was on her neck, teeth biting making her moan.

Hands in his hair, she said, "I've been wanting this since this afternoon."

His hands lifted her shirt and slid up her ribcage. "Your skin is so smooth and you taste better than the best sweets you could imagine."

"I thought you didn't eat sweets." She was having a hard time breathing when his fingers brushed her nipples through her bra.

"You have me rethinking that." His mouth finally came together with hers, his tongue immediately invading her mouth. She held on for dear life as they each fought for control. Kissing him was like diving off a cliff. Fast, with her heart pounding in her ears as adrenaline pushed her over. It had always been that way too. Their first kiss, when she was sixteen, had almost given her a heart attack. She hadn't been prepared for the rush and no one had warned her that a kiss could change her life.

But now she knew.

She knew that Wes was the only one who made her feel that way when they kissed. It had never happened with anyone else. Only him.

"Wes, please," she breathed out his name as his lips slid down her neck. She wasn't sure what she was begging for but she knew that she didn't want him to stop.

"Fuck," he swore and hiked her up so her legs were wrapped around his waist. "I can't get enough of you." He was back to kissing her and she wasn't about to stop him.

He was pressing up against her core and she could feel him, already hard under his pants. Somewhere in the back of her mind, she knew they shouldn't be doing this. They were in the storage closet of his restaurant. When it was open. There were dozens of people only one room away.

"I'm gonna hate myself for this," she said when his lips left hers, "but we probably shouldn't be doing this here."

His lips against her ear stilled. "What if I went and kicked everyone out?"

"While that is definitely a way to get me naked faster, that's not an option."

He lifted his head, leaving her skin missing his lips and tongue. "We've opened a box here that I can't seem to close." He loosened his grip and she slid her legs back so she was standing. "Now that I remember what you feel like, I can't seem to stop wanting you."

She smoothed her shirt down where it had ridden up. "I'm not complaining, not at all. Especially, since it's the same way for me. I was useless this afternoon. I almost came here at least a dozen times."

"I would have liked that." He was staring into her eyes like he could see into her soul. It freaked her the fuck out.

Dropping her eyes to the floor, she said, "This is just attraction right?"

He was silent for longer than should be, making her lookup. His eyes were unreadable, but just as he started to say something, they were both started by a knock on the door.

"Wes," Julia recognized the bartender, Sabrina's voice, "there are a few orders."

"Be right out," he said, his voice void of emotion.

"I guess it's a good thing we stopped."

"Yeah." He straightened his own clothes. "I should probably go."

She nodded and he turned the knob, opening the door. "I'll just go back out front with Avery and Dax." The mood had definitely changed and she wasn't sure why.

"Okay." He was already donning his apron and washing his hands.

She walked behind him until she reached the door. Keeping her eyes on the door she said, "I guess I'll talk to you later," and pushed open the door.

She walked in a daze to where Avery was sitting. Only she wasn't with Dax as expected, but Joy.

"Julia!" Joy yelled, holding up her arms with a beer in one hand. "Isn't this exciting news?"

"Very exciting." She sat and grabbed her half-full glass of beer and chugged it down.

"Okay," Joy said. "I see someone is having a bad day."

"What happened?" Avery asked. "Everything was fine a few minutes ago."

"I don't know what happened. One minute we were kissing and the next he was all weird."

"Weird how?" Avery asked.

"If I knew that, I wouldn't be out here talking to you guys." She dropped her head down against the table.

"Tell me everything you said," she heard Avery ask."

She lifted her head. "We were kissing and then I said we should stop because, well, we were in the restaurant. He agreed and he made a comment of wanting to kiss me since the last time. I agreed and told him how hard it was to wait to show up here until later. Then, I asked if it was just attraction, and that's when Sabrina knocked on the door."

Joy shook her head. "Oh hell. You don't really think that, do you? That it's just attraction?"

"What? I don't know. Why would that matter?"

"Because that's why he got weird. I don't want to break confidence, but I can tell you that to Wes, it is one hundred and fifty percent, not just attraction."

She froze in place. Was that it? Did he think she wasn't as invested as he was? Because that was not the case. Plus, that hadn't been what she was saying. She was only asking if the whole needing to see him and touch him and kiss him thing was attraction. Not their whole relationship.

She groaned and reached for Joy's almost empty beer, drinking it all down. "Why do I keep fucking this up?"

"You're not fucking it up," Avery said. "Relationships take work. Hell, I said the wrong thing a hundred different times when Dax and I first got together. It happens when there are feelings involved."

"So what do I do?" She was so out of practice. Really she'd never had any practice. Wes was her only real relationship, and that was so long ago.

"You march your ass back there and tell him what you want." Joy punctuated her words with a fist pound to the table.

Pushing back from the table, she stood tentatively. Taking a deep breath she gave her friends one last look before walking away. At the door that separated the restaurant from the kitchen, she closed her eyes and steadied herself. Opening them back up, she pushed open the door.

Wes immediately glanced at her before turning back to the food he was preparing. "You shouldn't be back here, Julia. It's against code." His voice was clipped, like the Wes of a few days ago. Not the Wes from today.

"Yeah well that didn't stop you ten minutes ago." She didn't move any closer even though she badly wanted to. "This thing between us, this relationship. It's not just attraction for me either. I didn't mean it that way. You confuse my brain and I can't seem to say the right things when you kiss or touch me."

He set the plate down that was in his hand. "You think I'm not confused? Julia, all I am is confused. You show up in my life after fourteen years and the feelings that I thought I'd done a damn good job of hiding, pop back up. And this time—this time—they are stronger and more powerful than I ever thought possible. Talk about confusion."

"Is it too much?" She clarified. "This. Is this too much?"

"I want to say no and keep having great sex, but maybe it is too much."

She didn't let that get her down. Instead she started to think like the therapist that she was. "Maybe we need to start from scratch. It's where most people start relationships, at the beginning."

"Can we do that? We already know everything there is to know about each other."

"Do we, though? Sure, we know everything from birth until we were nineteen, but do we really know these new people? The people who came after?"

"I guess you're probably right. So, we hang out and date." He finished with the plate he had been working on. "Although I have no idea when we will do that since I'm here twenty hours a day."

"We can figure that out." She moved when he opened the door and handed the plate to a waiter.

"I guess I'll call you then, and we can set up a time to go out."

She wasn't willing to wait for that. If she wanted this she needed to let him know. "What about tomorrow morning? We can have coffee before you have to be here."

He looked surprised and that told her that she'd done the right thing by asking.

"I like to be here by ten so what about nine?"

"Perfect. The bakery on Main street at nine. I'll see you then." She went to leave but stopped when he said her name.

"Just because we are slowing this down doesn't mean the attraction has gone away."

She smiled, pushed open the door and said, "Duh," as she walked through.

The attraction wasn't ever going to go away; she was positive of that. But, what she needed to find out was if she actually liked the man he was now. She suspected she did, but if they were going to do this, she needed to be sure. And so did he. She wasn't the naive, quiet girl she used to be. Now she was a confident, smart, outgoing adult. She might have forgotten those things for a few days, but it was time he met the real her.

Chapter 11

Sleep was not his friend. Not when all he could see when he closed his eyes was Julia, naked in his bed.

Yeah, this dating with no sex thing was possibly the worst idea ever.

He threw his covers off and sat up. It didn't help that he could still smell her.

Pansies.

It had always been her favorite, so at least he knew that hadn't changed.

Dropping his feet to the floor he picked up his phone. He'd had to stop himself a dozen times from texting her already, but this time he wasn't even going to try.

Texting was part of dating right?

It wasn't like he was asking for a booty call...not that he'd turn it down.

Wes:

Looking forward to tomorrow

He was shocked when her reply came right back.

Julia:

Don't you mean today? It's after midnight.

She was right, it was after midnight. In fact it was after one. He knew why he was still awake but why was she still up?

Wes:

I hope I didn't wake you

Julia:

No, I was up. Can't sleep.

Wes:

Me neither. Every time I lay down I smell pansies.

Julia:

Are you trying to get me to remember this afternoon?

Wes:

Was it that forgettable?
Julia:
Stop fishing for compliments. You know how good it was. I couldn't forget it if a doctor removed my memory.
Wes:
As much as I want to see you, that will have to suffice. I'll see you in a few hours.
Julia:
Hey Wes...this is hard for me too.

He reread that last text over and over again. It helped to know she was suffering too, but that didn't help him sleep. He'd learned years ago during therapy that when his mind wandered he needed to do something to keep it busy. That was usually running. But, since it was after one in the morning, he didn't think that was a great idea. Cedarville was a safe town, as safe as they got, but he wasn't stupid.

Standing up, he threw on a pair of gym shorts and his shoes. Since running was out, he had to find another way to quiet his mind and burn some energy. Since Joy was asleep, he popped in his earbuds and began doing sit ups, pushups and anything else he could think of that was quiet.

Thirty minutes later, he was finally tired enough to sleep. Shedding his clothes and shoes, he fell into bed and soon was out. Normally he didn't need an alarm to get up, but he'd set one anyway just to make sure he didn't sleep through his internal one. When he woke up at seven, he decided he could get a quick run in before their coffee. With his schedule, he never knew when a run would be possible.

He did a quick three miles, took a shower and still had time to throw in some laundry before leaving. When he pulled up to the bakery, he saw that it was packed, which he should have guessed since it was a Saturday morning. He was pleasantly surprised to find Julia already there and sitting at one of the outside tables.

"Good morning," he said as he walked up to her table.

"Hey." She looked up at him through her sunglasses.

She was casually dressed in shorts and a tank, which fit the June weather perfectly. "I can go grab us drinks if you want so we can keep the table."

She smiled. "I saw the empty table when I pulled in and figured I should take it since it's so busy."

"Smart thinking." She told him what she wanted and he went inside to order. Coffees in hand, he joined her back outside.

"How's your morning?" he asked, slipping on his own sunglasses. The sun was pointed directly at them and it was bright.

"Good. I went for a run which felt nice because I haven't run since last weekend."

"You run?" He was surprised. She'd always hated any form of exercise as a teenager.

She laughed. "Shocking right? Yeah I picked it up about the same time I came to terms with never being a size two. I decided if I was going to eat I needed to do something to combat the calories. Once I started though, I found that it was a great stress reliever."

"It is. I started running when I started therapy. My therapist said I needed something to quiet the voices in my head."

"He's right." She took a sip of her coffee. "I'm guessing you are a lot faster than I am."

He shrugged. "Speed doesn't matter. Doing it is the main thing."

"Says the man who has muscles everywhere."

"I like you just fine without the muscles. In fact, I might like you too much."

"Stop that. So, I know that you run. What else do you do for fun?"

"What's fun?" he mocked. "Since I moved here I haven't had a whole lot of free time."

"There has to be something."

"Like most guys my age, I like video games. Dax and I play whenever we get the chance."

"So running and video games. You're very well rounded."

"Are you making fun of me?"

"I think I am." She was laughing and he joined in.

"What about you? What do you like?"

"Let's see, I like to read...a lot. So much that it's a little obsessive. I think I did that more though because I could do it alone and didn't have to go out or be with people. For my first few years in Tennessee I was a real hermit."

"I'd say I'm surprised, but you were always shy."

"It wasn't that I was shy, it was more that I was nervous to be myself." She played with the mole on her hand. "Don't take this the wrong way, but it was also that I didn't have to be outgoing. I had you and I didn't need, or want, anyone else."

"I guess I probably should have pushed you to do more things without me." He remembered that, if she needed to ask something of someone, she'd always asked him to do it for her. And he'd done it because he'd loved her and didn't want her to be afraid or nervous.

"It wasn't your fault, Wes. I just used you as my crutch. But after a few years in Tennessee, I realized I needed to be more assertive and less fearful. Especially if I was going to be a therapist. So I started doing things that took me out of my comfort zone. It was hard at first but after a while I found who I really was."

He was amazed by her strength. "That's fantastic, Julia. You're amazing."

"I'm just okay." She laughed and took another drink of her coffee. "So I have a question for you?"

"Hit me."

"When we were naked yesterday, I noticed the roman numeral tattoo on your side. What does it mean?"

Oh hell. Of all the things she could have asked, that was not one he wanted to answer. "I'm not sure you want to hear this."

Frowning, she said, "That's a little ominous, and now I really want to know."

Sighing he set down his coffee. "They're dates."

"All right. What's so odd about dates?"

"They're dates of pivotal moments in my life." He was hoping she would let him leave it at that. He did not want to tell her the dates.

She eyed him speculatively. "Why am I sensing that one of those dates has something to do with me?"

He was going to have to do this. "The first one is the date you and I started going out."

A smile crept up her face. "That was a pretty important date for me too. What are the others?"

"Then there's one for my first year clean and my newest one for the day I closed on Dockside."

"All very important dates. But wait, weren't there four lines?"

Damn her and her smart, inquisitive mind. "There are four." In for a penny as they said. "The second line is the date you left town." He waited for her to explode, maybe get pissed but it never came.

"That makes sense."

"That makes sense? That's all you have to say?"

"What am I supposed to say, Wes? I know that I caused you trauma, and I know I was an ass. I can't be mad that to you that is a pivotal date in your life. It's important to me, too."

"I was so sure you'd be upset at me using that date. I guess you really have changed."

"The old me, the one who didn't know herself well and relied on you for everything, that girl would have been upset. But this me, I know and understand why you did it."

"The new you is pretty damn appealing." He thought he'd loved the girl he'd dated in high school. But this new Julia, he liked her. And that was more important. "So those are my tattoos."

"Are those the only tattoos you have? I don't remember seeing anymore."

"That's it. I was never really a tattoo person and only got the dates to help keep me stable." That made him wonder about her. "Do you have a tattoo?" For some reason that thought turned him on immensely.

She bit her bottom lip. "I have two."

"You have two and I didn't see them?"

"We moved kind of fast."

"Where are they?" He was practically salivating at the mouth waiting for her to answer.

"I have a small one right here." She turned and showed him her shoulder. On it was a small heart. "I got it to remember to love life."

He itched to reach out and touch it. Instead he took a sip of his coffee. "What's the other one?"

She stretched out her leg to the side of the table. She was wearing flip flops and he could see a flower tattoo on one side of the top of her foot. "It's a pansy."

"Of course." She loved pansies. "At least that hasn't changed."

"You do remember that I only like pansies because of you right?"

"You do?" He had no clue what she was talking about.

"It was winter homecoming our sophomore year. You had no idea that you were supposed to get me a corsage, and because it was last minute, the florist only had pansies left."

"Oh my God, that's right. I brought you a bouquet of pansies." He slapped his forehead. "I was such an idiot."

"I loved them though, and because of that night, pansies are now my favorite flower and scent."

"I don't think you ever told me that you liked them because of that."

"See, we still have a lot to learn about each other."

"I guess we do." They smiled across the table at each other.

"Should we do this again tomorrow?"

"I have a better idea. Let's go for a run together."

She shook her head. "I already told you that I'm not fast. There is no way I could keep up with you."

"It's not about that. It's something to do together that we both enjoy." He took off his sunglasses. "I don't mind running at a slower pace if it means I get to be with you."

"You really want to go running as a date?"

"I really do." He wasn't going to let her know, but he was turned on at the idea of seeing her run and get sweaty.

He was a sick man.

"All right, then it's a date."

"It's a date," he repeated.

They talked for another thirty minutes before he had to leave to get to the restaurant. He used the time alone to clean anything that was missed the night before. At ten-thirty Sabrina strolled in, a guy following her.

"Wes this is Patrick. He's the one I was telling you about."

He blanked for a second and then remembered they'd talked about hiring another cook. "Oh yeah. Hi I'm Wes." He shook Patrick's hand. "Why don't you come on back to the kitchen and we can talk." Wes wasn't sure who he was expecting when Sabrina had told him she knew someone, but Patrick wasn't it. He was way too clean-cut and well, perfect looking. He was wearing dress pants and an oxford. Honestly he reminded Wes a lot of Ryan.

"Thanks for meeting with me."

"I should be the one thanking you. Of course, I'd hoped that the place would be busy, but I never thought that after a week I'd need to hire another cook."

"That must mean you're doing something right."

"Let's hope." He pulled out two stools. "Tell me about yourself."

"I have a culinary arts degree and I've been working in restaurants since graduating eight years ago. Right now I am at Buchanan's in Woodridge, and while I enjoy it, it's a little more," he paused, "uptight than I would have liked."

"How so?"

"I want to cook and make people happy by adding my own flair to food, but at Buchanan's I have to follow strict recipes, and that's when I even get to make anything. Most of the time I'm stuck plating the food."

"That won't be an issue here. With a few exceptions, you could play around with ideas all you wanted. You do know though that this is a burger and fries kind of place."

"I do and I am fine with that. I thought I needed to go somewhere fancy to make a name for myself, but I am starting to realize that's not the case."

"Do you have to work today or would you want to hang around for a trial run?"

"I'd love to stay. I have the whole day off until six tonight."

Grabbing an apron and hairnet, he handed them to Patrick. "Let's see what you've got then. We open at eleven for lunch. Cook for about an hour or so and I can check you out."

There were some who would say that Wes was too kind and hired people on the spot but it didn't matter to him. He got vibes from people and that was enough for him.

"Here's the menu." He handed him a piece of laminated paper that held all the menu items. "The mac and cheese and jambalaya are my specialties, so I will deal with them. But, if you think you can handle it, I'll put you on everything else for the next hour."

Taking the menu, he looked it over. "I think I can handle it."

When eleven hit, people immediately started coming in. Saturdays were busy because of the lake, and this one was no different. Patrick worked hard as orders poured in. He held his own though, with no problem. An hour later, Wes told him he could leave but he asked if he could stay.

"I'm having fun," he said.

Wes agreed, and together they cooked for two more hours. A little after three they finally got a break.

"So what do you think?" Wes asked.

"I love it. I never get to cook this much and I miss it."

"I'm not sure I can pay you as much as you make at Buchanan's and I won't need you full time."

"Could I serve on the days I'm not cooking? I don't mind doing that."

"That's something you'd be interested in?" That was a surprise to Wes. This guy was good and shouldn't waste his talents just being a server.

"I'd really like to work here. This place is much more my style than Buchanan's." He looked down at himself. "This isn't me. I only dress this way because they make us."

Wes clapped him on the back. "Let's go get you an application and we can talk some more."

They went out front to the bar and while he filled out the application, they talked. They settled on him working the next two weeks anytime he could while he gave his notice to his current employer. When the two weeks were over, he would work weekends in the kitchen and once Wes was satisfied that he was fine alone, he would also take on one weeknight by himself. The rest of the time he would be a server and, hopefully, with tips, he would make enough to equal his current salary.

"Well, you did it again," he said to Sabrina once Patrick was gone.

"You can thank me by giving me a raise."

"Don't push your luck." He stood up and walked out onto the deck. There were a few people sitting at the tables and a few on their boats hanging out. A new boat was docking and he could have sworn he heard someone shout his name.

When he got a good look at the boat, he saw it was Leah, Carly, Joy, and Julia.

Smiling, he walked to the edge and helped them dock.

"While we appreciate the help," Carly said, "we could have done it ourselves."

"I'm ten thousand percent sure you could have." Laughing, he took each of their hands and helped them off the boat. Julia was last, and instead of letting her hand go once she was on the dock, he continued to hold on to it. She was wearing the same outfit she'd had on earlier, but now he could tell she had her swimsuit on underneath. Damn, he wanted to see that suit. "What are you ladies doing here?"

"Your brother is at my house making a giant mess and I had to get out, and thankfully, I was able to get a hold of these people to come with me."

"What?" Joy said. "I thought this was a genuine invite and now I find out it was only because Dax is disturbing your life? I'm deeply hurt." There was no conviction in her voice.

"Don't pretend to be mad," Leah said. "You know you wanted to come with us."

Joy rolled her eyes.

"You guys want food and drinks?"

"Can we sit out here?" Julia asked.

"You can. I'll send a server out." He reluctantly let go of Julia's hand and went back inside.

It was crazy how just seeing her made his whole day better.

He only wished they weren't on a sex break.

That would make the day even better.

Chapter 12

Julia wanted nothing more than to follow Wes inside. She'd spent an hour with him that morning, but it wasn't enough. She wanted to spend all her time with him.

Preferably naked.

But thanks to her big mouth, they weren't doing that.

She was a damn fool.

"You know, we aren't stupid," Carly said. "We know you want to go in after him."

She'd told them the whole story on the boat ride there. Everything from her showing up at Dockside Monday to what had happened in the kitchen last night. Plus all the sexy stuff in between. They all thought she was being ridiculous, but understood why she halted their sexy times.

"No, it's fine. I'm here with you guys and I want to be here."

"Bull. Shit." Joy said. "You are worse than Wes. I swear you're perfect for each other."

"I'm not sure I like having another loud mouth in this group," Carly said. "That's my job."

"I think you'll survive," Leah said. "Plus, Addison gives you a run for your money most days."

"I have to let her because she's pregnant. I can't be mean to a pregnant lady."

"Granted, I haven't known you long, but I'm guessing that doesn't normally stop you." Julia gave her a look that let her know she had her number.

Before they could continue a server showed up and took both their drink and food orders. Julia couldn't help herself and kept looking inside to see if she'd catch a peek of Wes.

Leah touched her hand. "Go see him. I'm sure he's in there waiting for you."

"I'm with Leah," Joy said.

She looked to Carly for her approval. Not that she needed it, but it would give her a little extra push to do it.

Even though she was going in to see him no matter what Carly said.

"Tell him we say hi."

Her last word disappeared as she jumped up out of her chair and walked fast inside. At the bar, she looked at Sabrina and she nodded that it was okay for her to go into the kitchen. Pushing open the door, Wes didn't look at her but said, "Five minutes. It took you five minutes to come and see me."

"I was having an internal battle with myself on whether or not I should."

"For future reference, the answer is always yes." He kept working on food and she stayed back so she wasn't in the way.

"Have you been in the lake?"

"Yeah, we swam off the dock at Leah and Brandon's before getting on the boat."

"I'm sorry I missed that." He was looking at her now, his brown eyes twinkling with mischief.

"Are you flirting with me, Wes Lange?"

"I sure am." He walked past her and pushed open the door to hand the plated food to a server. When he moved back he was standing close to her. He lifted a hand to her throat and she wasn't sure what he was doing, until he fingered her bathing suit strap. "Knowing you are wearing a suit under here is killing me."

"You've seen me naked."

"Yeah, but this is different. This is something everyone can see."

"Why is that different?" It was getting hot in there. She wondered if it was because she was in the kitchen or from the way Wes was looking at her.

Weren't they supposed to be refraining from this?

"Because when other people see you in a swimsuit they have to wonder what you look like underneath, but I know." His face was close and she could feel his breath against her neck.

She was seconds from saying fuck it and pinning him against the wall. Her throat was dry, so she had to clear it before speaking. "I don't think anyone is thinking of me naked when they see me in a swimsuit. I'm not exactly the size that inspires fantasies."

"Lia, look at me." She did as he asked and turned her head to look him in the eyes. "Believe me when I tell you that all men are looking at you. You are gorgeous and your curves only make you more so. You star in every single one of my fantasies."

Her heart was beating so fast she was having a problem breathing. He was so close now and she wanted nothing more than to kiss him.

"Why are you doing this to me?" Her voice was full of need.

"What am I doing?" He trailed a hand down her side.

"You're making me want you." She gripped his shoulder with her hand.

"Am I?" He searched her eyes. "Interesting." His hand traveled back up her rib cage until his fingers were just under her breast.

"You're doing this on purpose aren't you?"

A grin appeared on his face. "Maybe, but if it's mutually beneficial what does it matter?"

She shook her head and summoned all her inner strength to push him away. "You are the worst."

"And you like it."

She couldn't deny that. "I better get back."

He stepped back, moving out of her way. "I'll be at your house at seven in the morning."

She pushed open the door. "I'll be sure to wear something skimpy." She waved to him over her shoulder and walked back outside to her friends.

They hooted and hollered as she got closer to their table, making her hang her head in embarrassment.

"Stop it," she said as she sat down.

"You walked out here with the swagger of a woman who just got what she wanted," Carly said.

"I didn't *get* anything. We just talked." She took a sip of her beer which must have been dropped off while she was with Wes.

"Both of you are idiots if you weren't back there making out." Joy leaned back in her chair. "I miss making out. Maybe I should reconsider this guy sabbatical."

"There is a very hot, bearded, lumberjack who I am sure would make out with you."

"What?" Leah said. "Who are you talking about?"

"Dammit, Julia, that wasn't public knowledge."

She shrugged. "You make fun of me, I tell your secrets."

"Wait, wait, wait," Carly said, holding up a hand. "Are you talking about Flynn? The same Flynn who spends all his extra time at my house with Dax making noise and dirt?"

"The one and the same," Julia said.

"Flynn is hot," Leah said. "Did you see his body when he was at my party? I was drooling over him all night. That was until Brandon caught me drooling and dragged me inside to show me what I already had."

"That's where you guys disappeared to," Carly asked. "There were like forty people at your house."

Leah shrugged. "What can I say, my man loves me."

"Oddly," Julia said, "I kinda admire you for that. That's a bold move, having sex at your own party."

"That's what Brandon said." Leah began laughing and they all joined in.

"All this sex talk is killing me," Joy said. "I've already changed the batteries in my vibrator twice this month. Twice. I'm like a sex-starved maniac."

"Not to go all therapist on you, but if you were my patient, I would tell you that sexual release is perfectly normal. Everyone has a different sexual appetite and it doesn't make you sex-starved to want it a lot."

Joy looked at Carly and Leah. "Did Julia just give me permission to masturbate more?'

"That's what it sounded like to me." Julia froze. That was Wes. Holy shit, Wes had heard her talking about masturbation.

Fucking perfect.

"What do you think, Wes," Carly asked, "is excessive masturbation normal?"

Julia wanted to crawl under the table and hide. There were days where she wished she was still a hermit and didn't have any friends. This was definitely one of them.

"I am an advocate of self-pleasure." He glanced at her and held her gaze as he set plates down in front of each of them. "In fact, I use it often. Now, would I prefer a partner? Absolutely, but sometimes that just isn't an option."

Julia swallowed hard. She was getting turned on listening to him talk about masturbation. If this continued, she was going to fling herself off the dock and into the water, just so she wouldn't have to listen anymore.

"Enjoy your food. I have to get back to the kitchen." He walked away, leaving Julia wondering what the hell had just happened.

"Hey dummy," Carly said, "if you don't go after him, I will. And then it'll be a whole thing with Anthony because, you know, we're married, but I'm willing to risk it if it gets your ass out of that seat."

"But we decided that we needed more than attraction to make a relationship work."

"We love you, so we agreed with you because that's what friends do," Leah said, "but it's stupid. Attraction is how most relationships start."

"Go," Joy said. "Wes is giving you all the signs."

She stood. "I'm going but know this...if we don't live happily ever after, I'm blaming you." She walked away and tried to gather every bit of courage and moxie she could muster. Not even looking at Sabrina, she pushed open the door to the kitchen.

Only he wasn't there. She walked further into the kitchen when she was suddenly pulled into a corner and pushed up against the wall. His lips landed on hers in a furious kiss. It had only been a day since they'd had sex and then made the decision to cool it. But it felt like years.

She gripped his shoulders and pulled him closer. "I was stupid," she said when his lips left hers and took a path to her ear and then neck.

"You weren't stupid," he said against her skin. "You were right that we needed to get to know each other, but why does that mean we need to stop doing this?" She hugged his head to her chest.

"We don't, and oh God, please don't stop." His tongue was doing wicked things to her neck and collarbone.

"I wish I didn't have to stop this, but the next time I get you naked, I want more time to see you and cherish you properly."

She dropped her head back against the wall. "Why do we always start things we can't finish?"

He lifted his head and dropped a sweet kiss on her lips. "We're finishing this, it'll just be a few hours."

She took a deep breath and tried to stop her heart from jumping out of her chest. "Come by later. After work."

He had moved back a little, but his hand was under her shirt touching bare skin. "Is that okay? With your mom there?"

"Yeah, she'll be asleep and besides, I'm an adult and can do what I want."

"I'll text when I'm on my way."

She rubbed her lips together, stalling because she did not want to leave. "I um, I should get back out there."

Smiling, he leaned forward and gave her another kiss. "Think about me today. Oh, and take a picture of you in that bathing suit and send it to me."

"I'm not doing that!" She pushed him away, laughing.

"Fine. I'll just have Joy do it."

"You wouldn't?"

He started to walk away. "Wouldn't I?"

Walking after him, she shook her head. She was not going to take a picture in her swimsuit, and she was absolutely not going to send it to him.

Probably.

Wes pushed open the door and she followed him out into the restaurant and then outside. Grabbing his arm she pulled him back. "Don't you dare say anything."

He stopped, several feet from where her friends were sitting and turned to her. "Are you going to do it?"

She held his gaze, not blinking. He was half smiling and his eyebrows were raised. "Fine," she said in a low voice. "I will send you a damn picture."

He leaned in close, his breath hitting her lips. "That's my girl." Without kissing her, he turned and started talking to her friends.

She was stunned and couldn't move her feet to walk. First, he'd tricked her into taking a picture of herself and sending it to him, and second, he'd called her his girl. She wasn't sure which one was crazier.

Laughter finally pulled her from her thoughts and had her walking back to where her friends were chatting with Wes.

"What'd I miss?" Julia said as she sat down, purposefully not looking at Wes.

"Carly was telling us how Reed keeps asking where babies come from now that Addison is pregnant," Leah said.

"And what are you telling him?" she asked.

"That's the funny part," Carly said. "Anthony and Ryan freeze up whenever the subject comes up and end up telling him things like babies come from a virus that only women can get, to when people love each other, they can have a baby. It's funny to watch two grown men freak out over something so little."

Sabrina stuck her head out the door and called to Wes. "I gotta get going ladies. Duty calls." He gave her one last smoldering look before turning and walking back inside.

She didn't want to watch him walk away but it was impossible to turn her head. His ass was just as built as the rest of him and it showed, even in jeans.

Or, maybe especially in jeans since they were tight and fit perfectly to the curve of his fabulous ass.

"I hope to God you guys did the nasty back there." Joy's voice had her turning her head back to the table.

"I'm as progressive as the next person, but I don't think the health department would be okay with sex in the kitchen," Leah smirked at her.

"We did not have sex." She had wanted to. God, had she wanted to. "But, he's coming over later."

"So sex is definitely on the horizon," Carly said. "Those are some of the best days, early in relationships, when you know it's coming but have to wait all day."

"The waiting makes it hotter," Leah agreed.

"I didn't know death was hot," she deadpanned. For her the waiting was torture.

"You won't die," Joy said. "If anyone is going to die, it's me. I'm the only one not having sex here." She popped a fry into her mouth. "God, I seriously miss sex."

"Then have sex with the hot lumberjack and stop complaining about it." Julia shook her head laughing. "I don't know why you are in a self-imposed sex sabbatical ,but if you miss it that much, just do it. It seems to me you are trying to be someone you are not."

"But I," she lowered her voice, "I don't want to be a slut."

"That's why you aren't having sex?" Carly gaped at her. "That's stupid. If you like sex and want to have it, you should. Everyone else be damned."

"I'm with Carly," Julia said. "I already told you that sex is normal. Wanting it doesn't make you a bad person. As long as you're careful and protecting yourself, there shouldn't be a problem."

"That's just it though, I was being careless and that's how Avery ended up being attacked. I can't risk that again."

Julia softened, but before she could speak, Leah did. "I know what it's like to feel like you are the one who put someone in harm's way. Melanie got hurt because of some crazy guy who was after me. It was hell living with that. Until I learned that I was not the problem. He was. You have to learn the same thing. If a guy wants to get all pissed because you say no, even if you'd originally said yes, then they are the one with the issue. Not you."

"She's right," Julia said. "If a guy can't understand that then it's on him."

"I want to believe you guys are right, but I think it's going to take a while for me to get there. Until then, I'll just have to keep using my trusty vibrator."

"Take it from someone who went years without sex and only used her vibrator," Carly said, "there is no substitute for the real thing."

"Amen," Leah said.

Laughter went up all around.

They finished their food and then went back out on the lake. At one point, while everyone else was in the water, Julia took out her phone, found a pose that made her look better than normal, and snapped a pic. Then, before she could chicken out, she attached it to a text and sent it to Wes.

Not wanting to wait to see what he said, she joined her friends in the lake. Hours later, when they docked the boat at Leah and Brandon's, and walked up the path that led to the front of the house, she remembered the text. Removing her phone, she saw she had several new messages.

All of them from Wes.

Wes:

Why did I think this was a good idea? You are fucking gorgeous.

Wes:

Great, now I'm hard and I still have hours of work left.

Wes:

Don't ever doubt how hot or sexy you are. You. Are. Perfect.

She must have been smiling because Joy came up next to her and bumped her shoulder with her own. "Someone's happy."

"I am happy. It still feels so weird that Wes and I are together after all our years apart."

"That's because you're soul mates." She said it as if it was a given.

"Do you really believe in things like that?"

"I do, contrary to my sleeping around, I think there is one person in the world for each of us. Some find them early and some wait a lifetime. You and Wes...you were lucky. You found each other early."

"But then we lost each other."

"But now you're together again. Nothing could keep you apart."

She smiled again. "You know, I like you more and more each time we are together."

"I think that if I were into women, you'd be my soulmate."

"That might be the nicest thing anyone has ever said to me."

"I'm not sure if that's sad or good."

"Probably a little of both. I've never really had a lot of friends. When Wes and I were together the first time, I was shy and cared too much what people thought of me. Then I hid away for a few years and focused on school. When I finally decided to be this person, I was busy with work and trying to make something of myself. Plus, I never really found a group of women who I clicked with."

"Looks like you won't have that problem here. Cedarville doesn't seem to let people go friendless."

"It's kinda nice, isn't it?"

Joy looked back to where Carly and Leah were bickering about something. "It really is."

Saying goodbye to her friends, she headed for home. She'd promised her mom they would have dinner together, and while they were doing that, Julia planned to tell her what was going on with Wes. He'd always been one of her mom's favorite people, and even after she'd broken up with him, her mom mentioned him all the time. It took a shouting match for her mom to finally stop talking about what a great guy he'd been as a teenager.

She wasn't an idiot, she knew he was a great guy and she'd fucked it up. But now they had a new beginning and she was going to do everything she could not to fuck this one up.

Chapter 13

Wes had never cleaned quicker in his life. With thoughts of Julia filling his head, he did a quick wipe down of the kitchen and then did the same in the dining area. His staff always cleaned the tables and floors but he liked to go over it to make sure it was done correctly. He never had to worry about the bar because Sabrina was a perfectionist and liked things a certain way.

When he was happy with the way the place looked, he locked up and raced to his car. He wanted to stop at his apartment first to pick up anything he might need for the next day. The more time he could spend with her before Dockside opened again, the better.

He found Joy awake on the couch when he walked in.

"I thought you were going to Julia's tonight?"

"I am. I just wanted to grab my things." He left her where she was and hit his room, where he packed a bag with running clothes and work clothes. In the bathroom, he grabbed his toothbrush and the box of condoms under the sink. He didn't think they'd use them all, but with the way he was feeling, you never knew.

"See ya!" he said as he walked behind the couch and toward the door.

"Have fun!"

Once in his truck, he sent her a quick text letting her know he was on the way and then drove as fast as was allowed to her house. When he pulled up, he saw her sitting on the front porch steps.

Before getting out, he steadied himself so he wouldn't jump her within seconds.

But man, did he want to.

"Hey." He walked up to the house, looking down on her when he reached the steps.

"How was the rest of your day?" Her voice was seductively sleepy and had him wondering if maybe this was a bad idea. She'd had a rough week and he knew she'd barely slept.

"Busy." He sat down next to her, dropping his bag at his feet. "Normally I don't mind but tonight I had other things I would have rather been doing."

"I won't lie and say I didn't miss you, but I will say that work needs to come first." She tilted her face up to his.

Using one of his hands, he stroked a finger across her lips. "You look tired."

A smile appeared and her tongue dipped out and licked his finger. "Nothing a little hot sex can't fix." Her smile was evil and had his dick stirring in his pants.

Standing, he pulled her up with him. "Then, what are we doing out here?"

Rising up on her toes, she kissed his lips lightly and murmured, "Come inside."

Reaching down to grab his bag, he followed her inside. The house was a ranch and since he'd been there many times as a teenager, he knew right where he was going. Inside her room, he found it had changed a lot in the years since he'd been there.

Gone were the posters of teenage actors and musicians, and the twin bed with the frilly bedspread. Now the walls were bare with a few framed pictures here and there. Her twin bed was now a queen covered in a plush looking navy comforter.

As far as he could see, there was nothing left of the young girl he had once loved. This was all new Julia. The Julia he was dying to get to know more about.

"It's changed a lot," he said as he set his bag down.

"I'm not seventeen anymore." He heard her voice and followed it to where she was sitting on the edge of the bed. He finally noticed what she was wearing. Short – ridiculously so – shorts and a teeny tiny tank.

They looked like they were probably pajamas by how loose-fitting they were, and he could see through the top.

She was not wearing a bra.

Her heavy breasts were pressed up against the fabric, straining to get out, and he wanted to be the person who let them loose.

"You are most definitely not seventeen." He walked to the edge of the bed putting himself directly in front of her.

She was eye level with his crotch and there was no way she couldn't see how turned on he was. Lifting his hands, he traced the outline of her breasts through her tank. Her intake of breath had him looking at her face, where he saw her eyes closed and her mouth open.

Dropping to his knees, he used both hands to lift her tank. The desire to see her bare was so strong that his hands shook as he did so.

He salivated at the chance to take her in his mouth, and he didn't hesitate. She moaned when his tongue touched her nipple and one of her hands came up to grab his hair. He lifted one heavy breast with his hand and plucked at the nipple with his thumb and index finger while his mouth lapped at the other one.

Her fingers were gripping his hair hard as he continued to treasure her breasts. And it was treasuring. He wanted her to know that he loved them, and not to care if anyone else didn't.

He wanted to be the only one who mattered.

The fingers of his free hand began tracing her stomach. The skin was soft making him want to lay her down and kiss every inch of it that he could. When his fingers came into contact with her shorts, he struggled not to dip them inside and feel even more of her.

"Wes," her voice was heavy with lust, "I'm dying here."

He lifted his head from her chest and looked up at her. "We can't have that now can we?" Pushing her backward, her back hit the bed, but before he could climb on top of her, he pulled her shorts from her body. She was bare underneath, leaving him standing above her staring down at the sexiest woman he'd ever seen.

"Is this what we're doing?" There was a smirk on her face and he had to laugh.

"Oh no, there's more, but I needed a minute to appreciate your gorgeous body."

She blushed. "I feel weird with you staring at me while I'm naked."

"I saw you naked yesterday."

"But you didn't stare at me."

"And that's a shame. Your body is a work of art. And don't shake your head at me," he said as she was doing just that. "I'm the one looking at you, so I'm the one who gets to say how you look. And to me, you are perfect."

She opened, and then closed her mouth, and then frowned. "I'd prefer to look at your body," she finally said.

"That can be arranged." He kicked off his shoes and pulled his shirt over his head at the same time. Then he shucked his jeans, taking his boxers with them, leaving him completely naked with his erection bobbing in front of him. "How's this?"

She licked her lips and then bit her bottom one. "Much better."

He was done talking and needed badly to taste her. Falling back to his knees, he pulled her legs until her ass was on the edge of the bed. At her shocked face, he leaned in, intending just to breathe her in, but as soon as he got close he couldn't stop himself from placing a kiss right on her gorgeous pussy.

"I'm never going to survive this," he heard her say.

Saying nothing, he spread her legs further apart and licked down her center. She gasped, and because he loved the sound, he did it again. That was it for him. He couldn't hold back another second.

In an instant, he was devouring her with everything he had. She tasted magnificent, much better than he remembered, although they hadn't done a whole lot of oral when they'd been teenagers. It was one of those things that just hadn't seemed to matter too much once they'd actually had sex.

But, it had never been like this. And he'd never craved tasting her.

Maybe it was an adult thing. Maybe you only knew how great it was and how to really enjoy it as an adult.

He added a finger for more pressure and pumped it in and out. She was tight, almost as tight as she'd been at seventeen. When he felt he could, he added a second finger, and when she ground her hips down onto it, he knew he was on track to giving her an orgasm. Her moans stayed quiet but he knew that was because her mom was there. Yesterday at his apartment, she had been loud and he'd loved it.

"Wes," she begged quietly, "please."

He licked faster and pumped his fingers in and out adding a twisting motion to the end. Finally, he centered in on her clit, and right before he felt her go over, bit down, causing her to curse, and finally, come. He drank up her juices, slowing his tongue and then removing his fingers.

"What in the holy hell?" she said as he moved up next to her.

"That is my new favorite thing."

"Ah yeah, mine too." She sat up, breathing heavily and crawled down his body. "Although I'm thinking this might come out on top in a few minutes." Using one hand, she gripped his dick and ran it up and down.

"I'm gonna warn you now, I won't last if you put your mouth on me." There was no need to lie or try and hold back to make himself look good. He knew, without a doubt, that once her lips closed around him, he was a goner.

"Then I guess I better enjoy it while I can." Shifting her body again so she was between his legs, she kept up the pressure with her hand. That was until she dipped her head and licked the tip.

He sucked in a breath and his hand instinctively went to the top of her head. He tried hard to concentrate on not forcing her, but his hand, of its own will, pressed down. She didn't seem to have a problem with it though. She opened her mouth wider and took him in with fast bobs of her head. Then she slowed and used her fist to grip him tight as her tongue did wicked things to the head.

He was having a hard time breathing, let alone thinking, but for a second he wondered when the hell she'd learned to suck cock so well. But all thoughts went out the window when she took him deep enough for him to hit the back of her throat. When she choked a little, she immediately backed off but kept up the pressure.

He felt his balls tighten and when she took him deep again, he exploded in her mouth, a shout streaming from his mouth.

Realizing too late that he needed to be quiet, he grabbed a pillow and covered his face. The feeling of coming, let alone coming in her mouth, was too much to keep inside.

He heard her laughing and removed the pillow from his face. "That's not what I want to hear after you've just had my dick in your mouth."

She moved up next to him. "I'm laughing because you shouted and then covered your face with a pillow. I'm pretty sure the cat was out of the bag, so to speak, with the shout."

"I realize that, but it felt so good that I was afraid I'd shout again."

She laughed and leaned into his body. "Why were we so weird about doing that as kids, do you think?"

"I was wondering the same thing." He turned to face her too and ran his hand up and down her arm. "Maybe we were just so enthralled in actual sex that it didn't seem like a big deal."

"I guess." She shivered under his touch. "But we were idiots. Because that is something I want to do again. And soon."

Grabbing her by the back of her head, he kissed her. It was either that, or tell her that he loved her, and neither of them was ready for that yet. For minutes they just kissed. Yes, they were naked, and yes, they'd each just had orgasms, but that didn't matter. Kissing was enough. They were relearning each other and kissing was a big part of that.

As a girl, she'd been tentative when it came to kissing and always let him take the lead. As a woman, she didn't hesitate to be in control.

It was sexy as fuck.

It didn't take long for his dick to stir, and soon, her hand was snaking between their bodies, gripping it in her tight fist. Groaning, he moved his own hand down to her breasts. Her body shivered when he tweaked a nipple with his thumb and index finger, and when he did it again, she moaned loudly and pulled her lips from his.

"Condom. Now."

Jumping off the bed, he found his bag and hurriedly searched for the condoms. One in hand, he tore it open and slipped it on, while she sat up and watched.

"I don't remember ever watching you do that." She licked her lips. "I really missed out on a lot."

He moved back to the bed, dropping one knee next to her leg. "We have all the time in the world to remedy that." He leaned in further to her body, and when his cock touched her wetness, he pushed inside.

He kept his eyes on hers, wanting to see her face as he entered her. Her mouth was open and her eyes wide with pleasure. Fully seated, he didn't move, only relished in the feel of her wrapped around him.

Finally, when he could no longer take it, he began to move, Julia joining in, their bodies in sync. It had always been that way, and he had a feeling it always would. It was one of the reasons why sex with other women just hadn't been enough for him.

None of their bodies knew his like Julia's did.

Their breath mixed as each of them pressed harder and harder into the other, pushing toward release. He was afraid he was closer than she was, and because he wasn't going before she did, he rolled them so she was on top.

She sat up, planting her feet on either side of his body and slowly, moved up and down.

It was the best kind of torture.

His hands gripped her hips, fingers digging in to help steady her. He watched as she cupped her breasts in her own hands and held them as she rode him. Releasing one of his hands, he trailed it to her core and began rubbing her clit. When her head dropped backward, he knew she was close so he kept it up. In seconds, her body shook and her eyes closed as he felt her orgasm clamp around his dick. Gripping both her hips again, he pumped up into her furiously, the release so strong he thought he might blackout.

As his heart slowed, she dropped down onto him, her body like a blanket over his.

"I'm just gonna fall asleep right here," she said against his ear. "You're so comfortable."

Moving his hand to her ass, he kneaded the flesh continuously. "As much as I would like that, I need to get up and deal with the condom."

Sighing, she rolled off him.

He sat up quickly and removed the condom, before joining her back on the bed. She snuggled into his side and he wrapped his arm around her.

"Thanks for waiting up for me."

"If this is what losing a little sleep gets me, I'm game." Her fingers were aimless, running across his abs, making it hard to think.

"Did you get my texts? You never answered back."

"Yeah, I got them, and I didn't text back because it was embarrassing."

He moved to the side so he could look down at her. "I didn't make you do something you really didn't want to do, did I?" He never wanted to pressure her into anything.

"No, if I really hadn't wanted to do it, I wouldn't have. It was kinda...hot, knowing you wanted it and planned to look at it."

"I looked at it every second I could." He'd even been caught once by Ryan when he'd shown up to pick up some food for him and Addison for dinner.

"I'm thinking it's not fair that you now have a picture of me half-naked and I have none of you."

"We can fix that tomorrow when we run." He wasn't sure he could take it, thinking of her staring at his picture all day.

"I forgot," she said, lifting her head and scooting down his body. When her fingertips touched his ribs, he realized what she was doing.

"If I had to pick a tattoo for you, this would have been it." Her fingers ran over each line and he couldn't force himself to speak. "This date is so happy." He knew she was referring to the date they'd started dating. "And this one is so horrible." This time her finger moved lower to the date she'd left him. "But these two," she ran two fingers over the last two dates, "these are incredible. These are things you did all on your own and are huge accomplishments."

She looked up at him and the smile on her face made her look younger somehow. He swallowed the lump which had formed while she'd been talking. "The second one isn't as horrible as it used to be." He ran a hand over her hair. "I needed that to make the other two possible."

"I'm so proud of the person you have become," she said as she moved back up his body and laid her head on his chest. "I mean, I thought you were perfect at eighteen, but the man you are now is so far above that guy."

"You make me sound flawless and we both know that's not true. I'm just trying to be the best person I can be, and hopefully, do some good in what I have left of my life."

"If I'm the judge, then you are winning at the game of life."

"You're not doing so bad yourself." He chuckled and kissed the top of her head. "What you have done with your life, and all those people you help, that's above and beyond what most people would do."

He felt her yawn. "We should get some sleep."

"But I get so little time with you. I want to spend it all awake."

He slid her head off him and crossed over to switch off the lamp. "That will be changing soon." He pulled the covers up over them and repositioned her head on his chest. "I hired another cook."

"You did?"

"Yep. He's good too, so it won't be long before I will be able to have some time off."

"I love how hard you work but I won't complain about having a few extra hours to spend with you." She yawned again.

"Go to sleep. We can talk more tomorrow."

Sleepily she said, "Good night," and snuggled in closer to him.

For a few minutes he stayed awake and thought back over the years with her in and out of his life. At first it had been hard, the living without her. He'd numbed himself by doing more drugs. But the pain of her leaving was still there, making him realize that nothing was going to dull the ache she'd left in his heart. Getting clean had been hard. He'd failed more than once, but each time, it was Julia's voice in his head that made him keep trying. He'd heard her encouraging him and cheering him on. He'd thought of her standing by his side for years, in high school while he'd played baseball, and while he'd tried hard to keep his grades up.

She was his rock, even when she'd given up on him.

When getting clean finally stuck, he'd once again thought of her. Had she never left him, he might have never gotten clean. Her tough love, as hard as it had been to swallow, was just what he'd needed. Each day he stayed clean, he'd thanked her at the end of the night. It was his way of forgiving her, even though in reality, there'd been nothing to forgive.

Just like he had when he was eighteen, he loved her. She was it for him, and somehow, his heart had known it the whole time they'd been apart. Now he just had to find a way to tell her. Because for him, she was it. She was his future and he wanted to start that future now.

Chapter 14

It had been years since Julia woke up next to a man. And even more years since she'd woken up next to this man. Turning her head to the side, she saw that Wes was still asleep, completely relaxed with his arms stretched over his head. She smiled remembering their night together and turned her body into his.

He was such a different person than the one she'd known years ago, yet, in many ways he was the same.

The Wes from high school was brazen and bold. He never hesitated to talk to anyone or to try anything. While he wasn't unhelpful or ungiving, he never did things just because it was the right thing to do.

This new Wes though, was all about helping others and good deeds. And, while he was still outgoing, he was also reserved and a little shy. Especially, when it came to talking about himself.

She really liked the new Wes. She liked that he wanted to do good, and since that was her main goal in life, it worked that they had that in common.

Sliding her leg along his, she moved in even closer to him. He smelled good even after a day at work and a night of sex. Breathing him in, she closed her eyes and rested her cheek against his arm.

She felt him stir a little and then one of his arms came around her back. "Why aren't you still asleep?" His words were gravelly from sleep, but just hearing his voice had her body clenching with desire.

"Who can sleep when an exceptionally gorgeous man is in my bed?" Flirting wasn't something she was accomplished at, but with Wes, it seemed to come naturally.

"I thought we were going for a run this morning?" His free hand shifted and was soon fondling one of her breasts. While his words were asking one question, his hand was asking another one entirely.

"I think we can find numerous things that would get our hearts pumping." Her leg, which was between his, slid even higher as her hand skimmed over his stomach. His abs, which had been nonexistent as a teenager, were now one of her favorite parts of him. She loved the feel of her hands running over the deep ridges. There was something so stimulating about it.

"Are you trying to corrupt me, Miss Cahill?" Now his mouth was on her neck and his tongue was doing wicked, wicked things.

"I don't believe you need any coercion into being corrupted, Mr. Lange." Turning his face toward her mouth, she licked his bottom lip and then bit down lightly.

His gorgeous brown eyes went wide, and she loved that she could find ways to surprise him. She felt his hand move lower until it was between her legs, one finger entering her almost on contact.

She gasped at the feel of it inside her, a smile appearing on his face. "Looks like two can play this game."

Using her free hand, she gripped his shoulder, her nails digging into his skin. Dropping her forehead to his, she glued her eyes to his as his finger pumped in and out, pressure building.

She tried to remember to move her own hand up and down his cock, but it was hard to think while on the verge of orgasm. And, when he added a second finger, she forgot all about what she was supposed to be doing to him. Instead she kissed him, their lips connecting in one small movement. He tasted like sleep, and happiness, and so much more. If a kiss could tell the future, this one was telling her to hold on to him with everything she had, because together was how they were meant to be.

She came on a moan that he swallowed as her body shook. She was still coming down from her high, when she was flipped onto her stomach.

"Up on your knees," he said as she heard shuffling behind her. She obliged, and within seconds, his hands grabbed her hips and pulled her backward onto his waiting cock.

"Ahhh," she moaned.

He began moving, slamming into her one hard pound at a time. His fingers kneaded her hips as he kept up his steady pace. The slow rhythm was almost worse than a fast paced fuck. But she didn't need to worry. Wes picked up the speed. Soon he was fucking her so hard that her headboard was hitting the wall.

She felt herself climb towards another release, and when he pushed her down flat onto the bed still staying inside her, she went off. Now she was laying on the bed, his arms braced on the sides of her, thrusting deeply. That was until she clamped down around him, making him groan out his own release.

He dropped down on top of her and she loved the way his weight felt.

"Good morning," he said against her ear and then kissed her shoulder where her heart tattoo was.

"Waking up might not be so bad if I could do it this way all the time."

"We might be able to arrange that." She felt him roll off her and then felt him move off the bed. She was too worn out to turn her head, so she had to just assume he was removing the condom.

The bed dipped and his hand grazed down her back. "You naked like this isn't going to get us out of bed any faster."

She turned her head to look at him. "Who says we have to go anywhere?"

He smiled and leaned down, his lips lightly kissing her back. "As appealing as that is, I need to eat."

"Fine," she pushed herself to a sitting position. "If food is that important to you, then I guess we can eat." She slid her feet to the floor. "Do you want to shower?"

He tilted his head. "Will you be in there with me?"

"I thought you were hungry?"

He stood and grabbed his pants. The bathroom was in the hallway and no way was he going out there naked. "I am, but you just put a shower with you on the table. Showering with a naked woman always trumps food."

She bit her lip and shook her head. "You're a strange man."

He grabbed her around the waist and hauled her up to his naked chest. "You know, we have never had shower sex together." He raised his eyebrows.

They'd both lived at home after high school, during their freshman years of college. Sex had been doable, but shower sex..not really something they could pull off. Actually, if she thought about it, she'd never had shower sex at all.

"What if I said, I had never had shower sex?"

He tilted his head back, studying her face. "I would tell you that I haven't either."

She was shocked at this piece of information, but while she was embarrassed at her lack of experience, Wes looked happy.

"Why are you smiling?"

"I just think it's kinda crazy that neither of us has done that. It's almost like we were meant to do it together."

She was trying not to read anything deeper into what he was saying, but it was hard when his face was full of so much emotion. Was it just shower sex they were meant to do together or was it more? She hated questioning herself.

"I think that means we should give it a go."

Taking her by surprise, he threw her over his shoulder and walked out into the hallway. She was completely naked, her ass in the air and he didn't seem to care.

"Wes, I'm naked!" She kicked her legs and held on for dear life.

"As will I be, in a few seconds." In the bathroom, he dropped her back to the floor and immediately turned on the water.

"You're a madman," she said as he pulled off his jeans.

"Are you saying you don't want this?"

She looked down his body to where his cock was already jutted out from his stomach. She swallowed then looked back up to his face. "Don't let this go to your head, but get in the shower."

Laughing, he stepped inside, her right on his heels.

Needless to say, they didn't come out until the water turned cold.

It was another gorgeous day, and because of that, they were once again sitting outside for brunch. The town was packed with locals and tourists, but from what she had seen being back home for a year, this was pretty normal in the summer months.

They were just about to order when Addison and Ryan stepped onto the patio.

"Hey guys." She waved them over.

"Interesting seeing you two here together," Addison said.

"Addison," Ryan said, shaking his head.

"What, all I said was that it was interesting."

"You'll have to excuse her. The baby is making her crazy. And mean."

"It's fine," Julia said. "Why don't you guys join us?"

"We don't want to cramp your brunch," Ryan said.

"Yes, we most certainly do," Addison said, already taking a seat.

"I'd apologize for her," he said as he sat down, "but then I'd be doing nothing but that for months."

Addison didn't laugh but she did smile. "I am sorry for being so...abrupt. It's like I can't stop the words from coming out of my mouth."

"That's very normal with pregnancy," Julia said. "A lot of women say that they just don't feel the need to beat around the bush, so to speak, when they're pregnant."

"That's kinda how I feel. There's just too much else to worry about."

"The only person she doesn't snipe at is Reed?" Ryan said.

"Because he's good and gives me hugs." She frowned at him.

"I give you a lot more than hugs and you still snipe at me."

"Can't argue with that," Wes said.

"You know, if you want to chime in, I guess I'll just have to ask what the hell is happening here?" She pointed to both Julia and Wes.

Wes spoke before she could. "We aren't hiding anything from anyone." He reached over and took her hand. "Julia and I are together."

His thumb running over the top of her hand had given her confidence. "A lot has happened in a week."

"I can see that," she lifted her eyebrows, "but what's it mean?"

Ryan reached across the table and took her hand. "Leave them alone, Addison." His voice was soothing even to Julia. It was obvious he knew her well.

She closed her eyes and took a deep breath. "All right." She looked right at Julia. "But soon, I want info."

Julia saluted her just as Wes leaned into her body. "Do you girls really give details?" He said it low enough that neither Ryan or Addison heard.

She turned her head just a little toward him. "Apparently it's something they do here."

"I'd say to exaggerate the details, but I don't think that'll be necessary." He tapped her lips with his finger and then turned back to Ryan and Addison.

The man was right. She would in no way need to exaggerate anything about their time together. When she turned back to the table, Addison gave a knowing look that told her she knew exactly what Julia was thinking about.

"Wes, dinner was fantastic last night," Addison said.

"You guys went in yesterday?" Julia was sad she missed them.

"No," Ryan answered, "I just did a takeout order because Addison was too tired to go out."

"Have you had the mac and cheese?" Addison asked her. "It was to die for."

"I had it Friday night, and you're right, it is to die for. What did you have, Ryan?"

"I had a grilled chicken salad which was fantastic."

"Ignore him," Addison said, "he eats all healthy and shit."

"Just because I don't want to eat cheeseburgers day in and day out, doesn't make me weird."

"I'm with you," Wes said and fist-bumped him across the table. "I generally try to eat clean and stay away from fried food and grease."

"Oh, God," Addison said. "There's another one. Help us now."

"You'll really love this then," Julia leaned across the table, pretending to whisper, "he runs, for fun."

"Hey, you run too." Wes was laughing.

"Yeah, but I only do it so I can eat the bad stuff. You do it and still don't eat the bad stuff."

Laughter and conversation continued throughout their meal. When they parted ways, Julia told Addison she would try to stop by her house later in the day so they could chat.

"It's amazing how much I enjoy living back here," Wes said as he drove her home. "I really thought it would be weird or I would hate it."

"It's the same for me. But honestly, if it wasn't for Avery coming to see me as a patient, I might not have ever met all these wonderful people."

"Avery's one of a kind, and I'm thankful every day, as I know Dax is, that you were able to help her."

"Avery helped herself. She just needed a little guidance to get her moving."

When he pulled up to her house, he stopped the truck and turned off the engine. "What are your plans for the day?" He reached for her hand and held it in his.

"I want to check in with some of the people from my group therapy and make sure they are doing okay, and then I will probably go see Addison."

He turned her hand over in his and spent seconds staring down at it. "What about tonight?"

"Are you asking me if I want to see you tonight?" She dipped her head down so she was in his line of sight.

"I guess I am."

He was so unsure of himself and that made him even more desirable. "That's an easy one. Yes I want to see you."

Finally, he looked up at her, his chocolate brown eyes boring deep into her soul. "I never want to pressure you, but for me, well, I want to see you all the time."

"You're not pressuring me, Wes. I feel exactly the same way." She leaned over and gave him a kiss. "What if I come by tonight before closing, and then we can go home to your place together?"

"That's the best idea since shower sex."

"Play your cards right and you could have both." She opened her door and began to slide out, him letting go of her hand as she did. "I'll come by around eight."

She shut the door and gave him one last wave before walking inside. Closing the door behind her, she leaned against it and closed her eyes.

"You look happy," she heard her mom's voice, but even knowing it was her, she still jumped.

"You scared me half to death, mom."

Sorry, hun. I just heard you come in and wanted to see how you were."

"I'm good." She pushed off the door and followed her mom into the kitchen. "Was it weird for you last night knowing Wes was here with me."

Her mom waved her arm. "Not at all. You are a grown woman, Julia. Hell, by the time I was your age, you were already ten years old."

"I know, but knowing I have sex, and hearing it under your roof, are two completely different things."

"I didn't hear anything. I still had some of those earplugs I used to wear when your dad was alive, so I put them in." Her dad had been an awful snorer, which forced both her mom and her to wear earplugs when sleeping.

"Thanks, mom."

"I like seeing you happy." Her mom handed her a bottle of water. "It's been a lot of years since I've seen it."

"I was never unhappy," she said, twisting off the cap of her bottle.

"No, but you weren't happy either. You were just existing, and that's no way to live."

Wow, her mom saw a lot more than she'd realized. And, what she'd said was true. She had never been unhappy but for years, fourteen to be exact, something had been missing. It was obvious to her now that it was Wes, but for all those years she hadn't known that.

"He makes me happy." She put up her hand. "But before you start, I have no idea where this is going or what it will turn into. I'm just enjoying it while I can."

"As you should. Take it from me, hun, life is short. If I had known that I was only going to get your dad for thirty-five years, I would have spent a lot more time being happy, and a lot less being mad or unhappy."

Looking down at the table, she played with the label on her water. "I know losing dad was hard, mom, it was hard for me too. But I want you to know that I am so proud of you and the way you have dealt with your grief. You are a completely different person than the one you were when I first moved home."

"That's because I realized something." She sat down next to her and ran a hand down her hair just like she'd done so many times when she'd been a child. "I realized that his death didn't mean I lost him. I still have him in here," she touched her head, "and in here," she touched her heart. "But most of all, I have him in you."

She felt tears in her eyes. "Oh mom." She leaned in and wrapped her arms around her mom. They had talked a lot when her dad had first died, but usually not about how they felt about him being gone. It was always superficial, surface stuff. And the therapist in her had always known that one day her mom would open up in her own way.

Today was that day.

"Enough of that," her mom said, pulling back and wiping her damp eyes. "I want to hear all about Wes and what's going on with you two."

For over an hour they talked and she told her all about his life the last fourteen years, at least the parts she knew, and what he was up to now. Before they finished, she made a promise that she would take her by for dinner one night soon, so she could try his food and say hello.

She spent the rest of her afternoon making phone calls to her group patients to see how they were doing. It took longer than she'd anticipated because a few had wanted to talk. That was fine by her though because she wanted them to feel like someone cared.

When the work calls were over, she packed a bag, including a garment bag that held her work clothes, and left for Addison's. When she arrived, Ryan, Addison and Reed had just finished dinner.

"Reed and I will leave you ladies to your girl talk while we go play some basketball." Ryan kissed her goodbye, and he and Reed walked away.

Addison lounged back on the couch. "I'm exhausted. Why is it that no one ever tells you how tired pregnancy makes you?"

"I'm pretty sure they do."

"You're supposed to be on my side."

"What if I told you that during your second trimester, you will get all your energy back."

"I hope so, because feeling like this for the next twenty weeks is not going to cut it." She lifted her feet and spread them out in front of her on the couch. "Enough of me bitching. Tell me about you and Wes."

"He's...amazing." She told her about how they'd decided to be friends, and then how he showed up at the funeral.

"He knew you needed someone. That's a keeper right there."

"But, can I keep him? I don't know what he wants out of this."

"The big question is what do you want?"

"I want him. I want us together, and if it were my decision, we would stay that way forever."

"You know you're going to have to talk to him right?"

She sighed. "I know, but I just want to enjoy this, especially if it's all I get."

"Take it from someone who fought tooth and nail against love, you have to fight for what you want. Sometimes you might have to make concessions. But, if you do," she rubbed her stomach, "you might just get everything you want."

Watching Addison rub her stomach made her remember her mom's comment earlier in the day. She'd said she had been her own age by the time she'd been ten. If she and Wes had never broken up, she could have a child, or even more than one, right now.

It was something she'd never thought about at eighteen or even twenty-five. But now at thirty-four, she knew her time was limited and if she wanted kids, it had to be sooner rather than later. Was that something Wes even wanted though?

"Can I ask you something kinda personal?"

"I am an open book, ask away."

"Did you and Ryan discuss having kids before you got pregnant? I mean was it something you both wanted?"

"We did, and yes, we both wanted kids. I mean, he already has Reed to take care of, but having one who belonged to both of us was definitely something we wanted. Do you want kids?"

"I do. I kinda think I would make a good mom, but I'm already thirty-four. It needs to happen soon."

"I think I see what you are getting at. You are worried that Wes might not want kids, and even if he does, that maybe it's too soon to ask?"

"Yes to both of those things." She sank lower in the chair and tucked her legs under her butt.

"Let me ask you this, if Wes had never come back into your life, what would you have done?"

She pursed her lips. "I don't know. I guess if it came down to it, I would have one on my own."

"Okay, and what if again there was no Wes but you met a new guy. How would you handle that?"

"I'd probably give it a few months, but if I didn't see a future with him, I wouldn't let it go on any longer. Plus at my age, I think people tend to know sooner if the relationship is going anywhere."

"Then what's the problem?"

She frowned at her friend. "I thought I was the therapist here."

"You are, but I'm guessing sometimes you don't always see things the same way when they happen to you."

"You're right, I don't. I guess I'm just so afraid of losing him again that I can't see any further than today or tomorrow."

"If it's important to you, then you better get yourself some binoculars."

Laughter bubbled up inside her at Addison's words. "That baby is making you nuts, you know that right?"

"Do you think it'll go away or will I always be insane now?"

"I think parenting is the toughest job anyone can ever have and it's a wonder that anyone is sane after raising kids."

"And yet, millions of people all over the world willingly choose to be parents."

"Maybe we're all already crazy." She said it as a joke, but some days she was pretty sure it was true.

She stayed and talked to Addison for another hour before leaving for Dockside. She was going to try not to think about her future or what Wes wanted, at least for one more night. She knew she needed to address it with him, but for tonight she just wanted to be happy.

Tomorrow was soon enough for possible unhappiness.

Chapter 15

The place was still packed at nine-thirty even though they closed at ten. He might have to rethink the hours, at least for the summer if he wanted to please his clientele. But he'd think about that tomorrow. Right then, he wanted to quickly say hi to Julia, who had been there over an hour, and he'd only had time to talk to her once.

He pushed the door open and was surprised when he saw her behind the bar, helping Sabrina.

"Hey," he said as he moved up next to the counter, "what's going on?"

"Sabrina was swamped so I jumped back here to help out. I hope that's all right?" She handed a man two beers and then went to the computer to input the info on his tab.

"She's saving my butt is what she's doing," Sabrina said. "She's smart and catches on fast."

"Don't worry, I'm not making any cocktails, mainly just pouring beer and wine, and taking payments."

He was in awe of her. Not only was she willing to come hang out at his restaurant while he was working, but when it got busy, she was willing to step up and help out. That was rare to find in a person, let alone in the person you loved.

And yeah, he loved her.

Again.

He knew days ago it was headed in that direction, but he finally admitted it to himself when he'd dropped her off at her house that morning.

He knew it was inevitable, and really if he thought about it, he'd never stopped loving her. Joy had been right all along.

There was no one else who would ever mean as much to him as Julia did.

The problem was, he didn't know if she felt the same way.

He wanted to think that her jumping behind the bar when it was busy was a sign that she did, but he wasn't sure. It was in her nature to help out when need be, so deciphering her actions was impossible.

"Did you need something?" she asked, as she walked over to where he was standing.

"I was just checking on you. I still have several orders to fill and we still have," he looked up at the clock on the wall, "twenty-five minutes until closing."

"I'm good," she promised, a smile on her face. "This is fun. I've never tended bar before."

He leaned in to steal a kiss. "From the look of all the guys lined up, it seems like you're getting the hang of it."

"Wes Lange, are you jealous?" She was grinning ear to ear.

"Just remember who you're going home with." He winked and walked away. Yes, he was most certainly jealous. She was gorgeous and her smile was infectious. So he knew what all those men saw when they looked at her. But he didn't want to be that guy. He trusted her, and even more, she was only behind that bar to help him out.

Shaking his head, he got back to work. Twelve orders later, he was finally finished cooking. After wiping down his kitchen he went back out to the restaurant to see how it was going. There were still at least two dozen people finishing their meals or their drinks.

Julia was still behind the bar, chatting with an older gentleman and his wife.

She caught his eye. "Hey Wes, come here." She waved him over.

He stepped behind the bar and walked to the opposite end.

"Do you remember Mr. Johnson, our English teacher in high school?"

"Oh wow," he turned to the couple, "it's nice to see you."

"This place is great," Mr. Johnson said. "We've been here several times already, and I'm sure we'll be back again."

"Thank you, I appreciate that."

"Keep up the good work." They shook hands and the Johnson's got up and left.

"You're a hit," Julia said, when they were gone.

"Just because my old English teacher likes it, doesn't mean I'm a hit."

"Look around, Wes, it's after closing on a Sunday night and the place is still full. You've done something great here and the town knows it."

He dipped his head and shrugged. He wasn't a fan of people praising him. It felt weird. "How was your first and only night as a bartender?"

Her eyes went wide with excitement. "I loved it. It's fun talking to all these people."

He gripped her around her waist. "Have I said thank you yet?"

"I've been thinking of creative ways all night, that you can do just that."

"You two," Sabrina shouted, "no PDA on the floor."

"You know I'm your boss, right?" Wes didn't let go of Julia nor did he look away from her smiling face.

"But the bar is my space."

"She makes a good point," Julia said.

Leaning down, he feathered his lips across hers. "Ready to head out?"

"Don't you have to close?"

"I talked Sabrina into doing it for me."

"And remember you owe me!" How she heard them, he had no idea.

Julia was laughing as he pulled her out from behind the bar. Outside, the weather was still hot, but the breeze from the lake made it bearable.

"I wish I lived on the lake," she said as they walked toward his truck. "It's so calming to look out on it, and just take it all in."

He'd been thinking the same thing since he'd moved back home. Growing up, he'd grown up on the non-lakeside of town. As a kid he swore that one day, he'd live on the other side, near the lake. Only, all his money was tied up in the business. There was no way he could afford a house on either side of the lake anytime soon. Would that matter to her?

"Maybe someday, you'll have that house on the lake."

"A girl can dream." They reached his truck and he opened the door for her and she got in.

He didn't want to start doubting himself, especially since he just admitted that he loved her, but why would she want to be with him when he couldn't give her anything? It would be years before he could afford a house of his own.

Climbing in the truck, he tried hard to forget about what he couldn't give her, and instead focused on what he could.

"You had the customers eating out of your hands tonight behind the bar."

"I don't know about that. All I did was take a few orders and hand out beers."

"Take it from me, bartending is less about the drinks and more about your attitude. And yours was just what those people wanted."

"I bet you used to get hit on all the time as a bartender?"

He shrugged. "Some, but I was never interested." He gave her a quick glance. "Girls that pick up bartenders are not really my type."

"What is your type?"

He knew she was fishing, but he didn't mind. "Well, I like a woman who knows what she wants. One who doesn't hesitate to say, jump behind the bar of her boyfriend's restaurant and help out. Or you know, one who will drop to her knees as soon as we get home because she just has to have my dick in her mouth."

He could see from the side that her mouth was wide open as she tried to think of something to say.

"You're not usually speechless."

"I'm trying to decide whether to bend over your lap while you're driving or if waiting until we get to your place is better."

Of course, she said the last thing he would have ever expected her to say. It was one of the dozens of reasons he loved her.

"If you're trying to shock me, you've succeeded."

She laughed and unclicked her seat belt. "So you don't want me to move a little closer?" She began to crawl close, flipping up the center console – he'd never before been so grateful that it went up. "And maybe, touch you here." Her hand gripped his dick through his jeans, it immediately coming to life in her hand.

He groaned and tried to keep his eyes on the road. "I love that you are doing that. I only wish I could watch you do it."

"You keep your eyes on the road, and I will deal with this, mmm...pretty big problem." He felt her unsnap his jeans and slide down the zipper. His breath was coming out faster and faster as her small hand was sliding inside his pants. When she made contact with his already hard cock, he sucked in a breath and worked hard not to close his eyes at the feel of her hand on him. But, if he thought that was difficult, he was a fool.

When her mouth closed around him, he groaned loudly. "Lia, oh God." It felt amazing. There was no way he could drive while she was doing this. He'd crash. But somehow, someway, he continued to drive while her mouth bobbed up and down on his cock. He couldn't see her because he didn't dare take his eyes off the road, but just the thought of what she was doing, along with how it felt, had him coming. He kept both hands on the wheel and rode out the orgasm as she swallowed it all down. When her head popped back up, he finally let himself look over to her.

"You just fucking sucked me off while I was driving."

She gave him a small shrug and head nod. "Yeah, so?"

He put his eyes back on the road as he pulled into the parking lot where he lived. "See this is why I love you. You just do what you want."

She was silent next to him, her eyes wide.

He pulled into a spot and parked. "What's wrong?"

"You…love me?"

He smiled. So she'd heard that had she. He hadn't meant to say it, but holding it in was stupid when it was how he felt. "Got a problem with that?"

She shook her head and bit her lip. "No problem, especially since I love you too."

The air rushed out of him. "Thank God." Reaching across the seat, he pulled her into his arms. "I missed hearing those words. It's been too many years." He didn't wait for her to speak, and instead kissed her. Her lips were soft and pliant under his, but all intense, full of passion and heat.

Her hands were gripping his arms tightly when he pulled away. "How'd we get here?" she asked, her voice full of wonder.

"To my apartment?" He was confused by her question.

"No, here. You and me, together, in love." Her eyes were dancing with happiness.

"That's easy. It never left." He ran a hand down her cheek. "I never stopped loving you, Lia. You have to know that."

"As much as I tried to stop loving you, I couldn't. You were always in the back of my mind."

They just stared at each other for several minutes, smiling at each other. "We should probably go inside," he finally said.

"Yeah." She scooted back a little but continued to look at him. "The air in here is thick."

He smiled bigger. "That's because not five minutes ago you had my dick in your mouth."

She rolled her eyes. "Way to be crude and ruin a beautiful moment." She began to open her door. "I was thinking of doing it again later, but now, I'm not so sure."

"No worries," he opened his own door. "I plan to spend several hours with my face between your legs." He stepped outside. "I have years to make up for."

He saw her shake her head as he closed his door. Meeting in front of his truck, he took her bags from her and reached for her hand.

Since he saw Joy's car in the lot, he knew she was home, but when they entered the apartment, she was nowhere to be seen. He'd texted her earlier to let her know that Julia would be coming home with him, so he assumed she took the hint and was hanging in her room.

"I guess Joy's not here?"

"I think she's in her room." He pointed down the hallway to the closed door.

"Oh. She didn't have to do that."

"We have limited time together, and while I like Joy, do we really want to spend any of our time with her?"

She tilted her head. "I guess not."

He flipped off the lights and guided her down the hall to his room. Turning the lamp on, he dropped her bags next to the bed. She sat down and started removing her shoes, so he did the same.

Once he sat down though, he realized how tired he was both, physically and emotionally. Holding in his feelings for her had been exhausting. When he yawned, she gave him a sideways glance.

"Tired huh?"

"Just a little."

"Thank God." She dropped back onto the bed. "I'm so tired, but I wanted to be with you so bad that I was trying to hide it."

He chuckled. "So we were both willing to give up sleep to be together. Must be love."

She reached above her head, found a pillow and threw it at him. From her position lying down, she stripped off her shorts and pulled her t-shirt over her head, leaving her in only a bra and panties. Suddenly he wasn't so tired.

"You know," he said and crawled on top of her, "I can spare a few minutes of sleep." He kissed her skin above her bra, and then higher, until he found her lips. It wasn't furious or urgent like their previous kisses. This was slow and sensual, the kind of kiss you have when you love someone.

His hands skimmed down over her ribs and he felt her skin pebble with goosebumps. He began to trail his lips from hers down her body. He stopped at her breasts, pulling the fabric of her bra down in order to touch skin. After slowly loving each breast, he kept moving down, ribs, belly button, and finally, panties. He kept them where they were, but continued to move downward. He saw how wet she was, even through the fabric, and fuck if it wasn't hot.

He leaned in and kissed her through the panties, loving how she moaned out his name. Slipping his finger between the fabric and her skin, he slid it inside and felt just how wet she was. She pushed down on his finger, forcing it inside and moaned loudly.

Taking his time, he began to lower her panties as his finger slowly moved in and out of her. He had to remove it for a second, and when he looked up to her face, he saw she was not happy about that. Grinning, he re-inserted it, while at the same time, lowering his mouth to her.

"Holy hell," she said, when his tongue licked her up and down.

He loved this. He loved knowing that she was at his mercy, and that he had complete control over her orgasm. It was the same when she sucked him off. Her having that kind of power was somehow freeing.

Her hands found his head and strong fingers pulled at his hair. He knew she was close, and sure enough, her body clamped around his finger. He looked up to her face as she rode out her orgasm and was rewarded with a smile of pure pleasure.

Sliding back up her body, kissing every inch as he went, he withdrew his finger from inside her. She turned her head to the side, and without any hesitation, let him kiss her with a mouth that was still covered in her juices.

"You do good work when you're tired." She was running her fingers ever so slowly through his hair.

"I don't think it will ever matter how tired I am, I think I will always want you." He found the covers with his feet and kicked them up and over them.

"I'm still in shock that we have found our way back together after all these years, and that somehow, we both want the same thing."

"Love will find a way, don't you think?" He yawned, making her do the same.

"Seems like it." She turned so he could spoon her from behind. "I love you."

Kissing her shoulder, he said, "Love you too. Get some sleep."

After dropping Julia at Dockside to pick up her car for work, and because it was Monday and he was closed, he texted Dax to see where he was working, and if he had time to talk. Dax answered immediately saying he was at Tony and Carly's for the final push of their new master suite and bathroom. Wes headed there and found his brother alone upstairs.

"Isn't this your day off?" Dax asked. "Why are you up and moving so early?"

"I had to drop Julia off at her car so she could go to work."

"That's going well then? You and Julia?" Dax set his tools down and reached for the coffee Wes had brought him.

"If being in love is well, then yeah, we are doing pretty well."

"Why don't you sound happy about this?"

Wes had been dreading this moment for years. The moment he told the people closest to him about what really happened between him and Julia. Both his mom and Dax had always assumed he'd been the one who started them on drugs, and rightly so. He was the outgoing one and Julia was the good girl. They'd both been angry that he'd let her go and didn't try to fight for her. He knew telling them would give them a different impression of her, and he didn't want that. But, it had to be done.

"If you have a few moments to spare, I have something I need to talk to you about."

"Do we need to be sitting for this?" Dax raised an eyebrow to him.

"Probably, but let's just do it here." He swallowed. "Remember when Julia and I broke up and I told you that I broke it off with her? Well, that wasn't entirely true. Actually it wasn't true at all. She broke up with me."

"Wes, you can stop right there. I already know what happened."

"What? How?"

"Julia told Avery and Avery told me."

Dax didn't seem angry or upset, so maybe it wasn't as bad as he thought. "Why didn't you say something?"

"At first, I was pissed. At her, not you. She got you into drugs, and then when you needed her, she upped and left. That's beyond despicable. I mean, who does that? But, Avery being Avery, talked me down from my anger. Once I had time to think about it, I realized why she had done what she'd done. You were gone back then. Not listening to anyone or even thinking you had a problem. And Julia, once she got clean, she had to do what was best for her survival. So I get it. I do. Honestly, seeing each of you now and how you both came out the other side so well, I think her leaving might have been for the best."

"I realized yesterday that I never stopped loving her. Not once. She was always there in my head, and in my heart, and I can't believe she still loves me."

"She's a good person, Wes, and also, she's not an idiot. You are the best guy I know, give or take a few years that you were seriously fucked up."

"Thanks." He took a sip of his own coffee. "I have another problem."

"Fixing things is what I do, so let's hear it."

"She wants a house of her own, a lake house, and there is no way I can afford that. Everything I have is tied up in Dockside, and it will be years before I have extra money to afford a house."

"Did she tell you she wanted a lake house?"

"She said it had always been her dream and that she was thinking of buying one."

"So what's the problem?"

"I can't buy it for her."

"What is this, nineteen-twenty? Bro, if she is going to buy herself a house, she doesn't need you to do it for her."

"But what do I bring to the table? Nothing. I have nothing."

"That's not at all true. You own Dockside outright. That's huge."

"I guess, but still I have no savings, because I used every penny I had to buy it."

"You bring yourself." They both turned their heads at the intrusion of a female voice. It was Carly. "I didn't mean to eavesdrop—well, actually yes I did—but Julia doesn't need anything from you. She just needs you."

"You say that," Wes said, "and yeah I know it's archaic, but the man is supposed to provide."

"And you will," Carly said. "You will provide for her needs in other ways. Hell, you own a restaurant ,so she will never want for food, and you love to cook, that's huge. Then, there are things like showing up at the funeral just because you know she needed someone. I don't think you know how big that was."

"Carly's right," Dax said. "The things that matter are not the things that money can buy. If she loves you, you being able to afford a house won't matter to her."

"I hear you, and I know you are right, but I still feel like a failure."

Carly touched his arm. "Do me a favor? Talk to her before you decide you are a failure. Because, if this were Tony and me, I would want to know how he was feeling."

He nodded. "I will, I promise."

He left feeling better, but still not one hundred percent sure how to feel or what to do. So he did what he always did when he needed to think. He took a run.

He was four miles in before his brain finally registered that Julia wasn't the kind of person who needed a man to provide for her. She had made it fourteen years on her own and had done pretty damn well. Yes, he wanted to take care of her, but that was on him, not her. And Carly was right, he needed to talk to her.

After a shower and some laundry, he headed to Dockside to deal with payroll along with other paperwork. He liked to work at the bar, and that's where he was when the door opened and one of the kids he'd met at the funeral walked in.

"Hey, good to see you," he stood and shook hands with the young man who's name he remembered as Jimmy.

"I hope it's okay that I stopped by. I didn't realize you weren't open today."

"Not a problem. Come sit." He pulled another stool out from the bar for him. "Are you hungry or thirsty?"

"Nah, I'm good."

"What brings you by today?"

"I was wondering if the offer of a job still stood? I brought my resume," he slid a piece of paper over to him, "but there's not much on there. I've only had a couple of other jobs and most of them were when I was using, so I'm pretty sure they won't give me good references."

Wes lifted his hand to the young man's shoulder. "Don't worry about it." He set the sheet of paper down. "Let's just talk. How old are you?"

"Twenty-one."

"And where do you live?"

"I live here in Cedarville with my mom. I used to live in Shelton with my dad, but that's what got me into trouble."

Shelton was about an hour north of Cedarville, and from what Wes remembered, it was a pretty drug infested town. "How long have you been clean?"

"Almost two years." His face lit up in a smile, one that Wes remembered well in those early years. The feeling of accomplishment was a huge ego boost.

"Congratulations. That's a huge deal."

"It feels good."

"It should. You've done something that a lot of people can't do."

"I don't want who I was to define who I want to be. Before drugs, before addiction, I had plans. I wanted to be a photographer or maybe a graphic designer. But now, I would just settle for a job."

"I think I might be able to help with both of those. Let's start with the job. First, is being around alcohol okay?"

"Yeah, I don't drink just because I don't want to chance triggering anything, but alcohol wasn't my addiction."

He nodded. "My bartender, Sabrina needs a barback, do you know what that is?"

"The person who gets ice and stuff?"

"Yeah, and also washes the glasses and clears the bar of food or garbage. Basically, anything but serving the drinks or food."

"I can do that." He looked eager and more than willing to work.

"I can't pay you much but let's start at twelve dollars an hour. If it works out, we can talk about upping it more later on."

His eyes were wide. "That's more than generous." They talked more about hours and decided he would work four nights a week, Thursday through Sunday. At least to start.

Jimmy left, a happy smile covering his face. Wes felt incredible that he was partly responsible for that smile. Giving back had always been something he'd loved doing, but recently because he'd been busy, he'd put it on the back burner.

But no more. It felt too good to help people, and he wanted to feel this way all the time.

Chapter 16

Elated. That's how Julia had felt all week.

She and Wes were in love.

In love, and spending all the extra time they had together, including nights.

But, it was more than that.

On Tuesday, he'd stopped by her office, bringing her a coffee and muffin before he opened for the day. On Wednesday, she stopped into Dockside for a long lunch, spending much of it in the kitchen with him.

On Thursday, he showed up again at her office, only this time, during her group session. She was concerned that he needed to be at the restaurant, but he assured her that Patrick – who had the day off from his current employer but came in to get acclimated – could handle things just fine for an hour or two.

It was finally Friday, and she was on her way to meet her friends for dinner and drinks. Afterward, she would swing by Dockside to see Wes.

She found a parking spot at the restaurant that they were meeting at and quickly gathered her purse and phone. She was running a little behind because her last appointment had run over. She never rushed her clients when they felt like they needed to keep talking. It might not be the most beneficial thing for her bank account, but it was the right thing to do.

Entering the place, she looked around and spotted Carly, Addison, Leah, Melanie, Avery and Joy all gathered around a table. "This looks like trouble," she said as she hung her purse on the back of the only empty chair.

"Julia!" Avery shouted and then stood up to give her a hug. "Where have you been? Carly has a story to tell us, but wouldn't tell it until everyone was here."

"Sorry. My last appointment ran a little late." She pulled out her chair and sat right as the waitress came over to the table. She ordered her drink while a few ordered a second. "I'm here now so you can feel free to tell this amazing story."

Carly, who was always confident and never shy, looked a little bashful. "It's not really a story so much as a piece of information." Her eyes glinted a little in the dark restaurant. "I'm pregnant."

"I knew it!" Mel shouted. "Headache my ass."

Everyone stood up to hug their newly pregnant friend. Julia nudged Joy and said, "Headache?"

"Carly told us she wasn't drinking tonight because of a massive headache." As excuses went, it was a good one.

Hugs over, they all sat back down and Leah asked, "When did you find out?"

"Just this morning. As most of you know, I went off the pill on our honeymoon, so we were trying. When I woke up three mornings in a row slightly nauseated, I decided to take a test."

"You're just barely pregnant then," Julia said. "Maybe four weeks?"

"That's what I'm assuming. I took four tests just to be sure because, well because I'm anal like that. But I guess I'll go to the doctor next week, just to have it confirmed."

"Is Tony through the roof?" Addison asked. "He has to be."

Carly smiled. "He's beyond excited."

Julia listened to all the talk about babies, the whole time wondering if a baby was ever in her future. She was the oldest one there, and yet, other than Joy, the only one who had no idea what her future held. It was too soon to ask Wes where they were headed, even though she wanted to believe he was in the same place as she was.

But, how did you ask a guy you just started dating if he wanted to have kids? And would asking him make him run?

Some days she wondered how relationships lasted with each person's insecurities bubbling up and taking over a brain that knew better.

When dinner with her friends was over, she headed to Dockside. Halfway there, she changed her mind and went home. She needed time to think, and if she was near him, all rational thought went out the window.

She didn't want him to worry though, so she texted him.

Julia:

Decided to come home after dinner, hope that's ok.

Wes:

Already sick of me, huh?

Julia:

Not at all. Just need a little me time.

Wes:

I understand that better than anyone, Lia. Want me to come by when I close or do you want to be alone?"

Julia:

That's a stupid question. Come by.

She wasn't an idiot. Needing to think was one thing, but sleeping alone...that wasn't something she ever wanted to do again.

At home, she settled in her room with her laptop on her lap. She was ready to start her future and that meant it was time to move out of her mom's house. She wasn't wealthy, far from it, especially after almost depleting her savings when she had to buy out her contract in Tennessee. But, she still had a little left. Not to mention she had worked for over a year at her new practice and didn't have to pay a penny in rent or utilities. The money had started piling up and now she had a nice nest egg.

Enough that she could put a down payment on her dream house.

Logging onto her computer, she pulled up a realtor site. She began scrolling through the houses, not really paying attention. That was, until one caught her eye.

It was everything she wanted. Three bedroom ranch with three bathrooms and a finished basement. The ceilings were vaulted, and instead of separate dining and living room areas, it was one great room.

The only problem...it was way out of her price range.

She could afford the down payment, but she knew for a fact she would struggle with the monthly bills. If she could somehow swing it, she would be house poor, and she wasn't sure that's what she wanted.

Shutting her laptop harder than she should have, she slid down the bed and turned on her side. She wanted that house, but she also wanted kids. Not to mention Wes. She most certainly wanted him.

Was there a way to have it all? Was that just a pipedream? Did anyone really have it all? She wasn't sure of the answers, but she knew one thing. She wanted to try.

She could only have it all if she took chances, and that meant she needed to talk to Wes.

But she couldn't do that until she saw him, and that wouldn't be for hours yet. Snuggling even deeper into her bed, she let her eyes close.

The next time she opened them, it was dark in her room and there was a warm body wrapped around her.

"Wes?" she said sleepily.

"Go back to sleep," he told her and kissed the back of her head.

She wanted badly to say no and wake up to talk, but she was tired, and what was the harm in waiting to talk until the morning?

Craziness. That was the harm.

Both she and Wes were awoken at four in the morning when each of their phones were going off.

"What the fuck," Wes jumped from the bed and reached for his phone.

As he answered his, she finally found hers and saw it was Leah.

"Leah what's wrong?" It was four in the morning. There was no way she was calling with good news.

"Is Wes there?"

"Yeah, he's on the phone." When she looked over at him, she saw that his face was blank and he wasn't speaking, but his phone was still pressed to his ear. "What's wrong?"

"There was a fire at Dockside. Brandon's there now."

"What!" she shouted and Wes turned toward her, realizing she too was on the phone.

"It's not bad from what Brandon says but he needs Wes to get down there."

"I'll bring him." She hit end and dropped her phone just as Wes was getting up. "Was that Brandon?"

He was frantically dressing. "A fire. There was a fucking fire. How is that possible?"

"I don't know," she said as she pulled on shorts. "But, let's not freak out until we see it."

He stopped moving when she put her hand on his shoulder. Turning, she saw how full of emotion his eyes were. "It's going to be okay."

He took several deep breaths. "I need you to keep telling me that. I'm not sure if I'm strong enough for this."

"You are." She ran her hand down his chest. "And if you feel like it's too much, lean on me. I can take it."

They finished dressing, and in record time, she drove them to Dockside. When they pulled into the parking lot, it was filled with several fire trucks and police cars. They found Brandon immediately inside the door.

"Hey guys," he said.

"Where was the fire?" Wes said. His voice was calm, but she knew he was anything but.

"From what the fire department can tell, it started out back in the dumpster and spread into the kitchen."

"It wasn't one of the ovens?" Julia kept her hand in his for support as he asked his questions.

"Nope, but why don't you go talk to the fire chief." Brandon pointed him out to Wes and Julia let go of his hand as he started to walk away.

"This blows," she said to Brandon after he was gone.

"Yeah, but at least, since it looks like it wasn't anything he did, insurance should cover it."

It occurred to her then that she didn't know anything about Wes and his finances. How had he afforded this place to begin with? It couldn't have been cheap and remodeling and running it had to have cost a pretty penny.

She wasn't sure what to do while she waited for him, so she went outside and stared at the lake. This was the worst thing that could have happened to him after he'd worked so hard to get the place up and running. She wanted to help, but had no idea how. She wasn't sure how long she'd been standing there when he came up behind her.

"We can go whenever you're ready."

Turning she looked up at him. "How bad is it?"

"It could be a lot worse. It's just the back of the kitchen, but that's the whole wall, including food storage, supplies and the whole prep area. None of the big grills were ruined thankfully but it's still a ton."

"I'm so sorry, Wes."

He sighed and dropped his forehead to hers. "If you weren't here, I don't think I could deal with this."

"Lean on me all you want." She reached for his hand, gripping it tightly in hers. "I'm here for anything you need."

"Right now, I just need to get a few more hours of sleep with you by my side."

They made their way out front and into her car. As she drove them home, her mind kept wandering back to right before she had fallen asleep that night. Or the night before. None of that seemed to matter anymore. She wanted a house, yes, but she wanted Wes more. And she knew deep down that he could not afford to help her buy that house she loved so much. Probably not before, but definitely not now that his business needed his extra money.

She'd give every penny she had to him if it meant helping him keep his business.

Back at her house, they crawled into bed, Wes snuggling up behind her. "Thank you for being with me tonight."

Threading her fingers through his on her stomach, she said, "I love you."

When she woke up, she found Wes still fast asleep. Not wanting to wake him, she dressed quietly, grabbed her phone and headed to the kitchen. Her mom was nowhere to be seen, but since coffee was already made, she assumed she was up and on her morning walk. Grabbing a cup of coffee, she took a seat at the table and texted Avery.

Julia:

Did you hear what happened last night?

Avery:

What?

Julia:

There was a fire at Dockside.

Her phone rang.

"What?" Avery shouted as soon as she said hello. "A fire? Was anyone hurt?"

"No, it was after hours, but it did do some damage."

"Well hell, what happens now?"

"I don't know. Hey Avery can I ask you something?"

"Anything."

"How did Wes afford Dockside?"

"Oh. It was like all the stars aligned perfectly. The previous owner had called Dax to see about doing some work so he could sell it. Dax mentioned it to Wes and, of course, when Wes saw it, he loved it. So instead of having work done, the owner sold it as it was, for a low price. Wes was able to buy it outright without getting a loan. He had just enough left over to pay for the materials for the remodel. Dax did the work for free, which helped a ton."

"Wow, I had no idea."

"Yeah it all worked out perfectly. This is a huge setback."

"Seems like it might be." But she had an idea. "How fast can you get dressed and meet me?"

"Pretty fast since I'm already dressed. Where are we meeting?"

She bit her lip. "I don't know."

"Come here. Dax is working, although I have to guess when I tell him about Dockside, he will head to wherever Wes is so he can help."

"That's just what we're going to do. I'm on my way. Do me a favor, text everyone else and see who can meet us."

"You got it."

Julia scribbled Wes a note and then tiptoed back into her room to leave it for him. She wanted him to know where she was and for him to join when he was ready.

As she drove to Avery's, she began to rethink her future. Last night she had been so sure she needed that house to be happy. But now, she knew that what she needed was just Wes. But, a Wes who was happy and had all the things he wanted. That meant, that as the person who loved him, she had to see to it that he had everything he wanted.

She recognized Leah's car when she pulled in and found her already inside with Avery.

"Listen, if we have to kill someone, can we do it quickly? I have to be at the studio in just over an hour."

"We aren't killing anyone. Although if Brandon gets any hits on who the hell started a dumpster fire, that person is first on my list." She sat down at the counter, pulling out her laptop as she did. "I need to come up with a way to help Wes get Dockside back up and running quickly."

"Brandon is beside himself that this happened. He feels like he let Wes down."

"Unless he was staking out the back of the restaurant, there is no way he could have seen this coming," Avery said. "Dax said whatever you need from us, we are in."

"I just don't know the best way to go about this. I know it will be at least a few weeks before insurance will get him his money, but I don't think he can wait that long. He will lose a ton of business, not to mention the employees will lose money because they can't work."

"That's the good thing about having friends, we are all willing to help. Brandon has the weekend off and I'm in too, after noon, when the studio closes. I know Carly and Mel, along with Tony and Logan, will help too. I think with all of us we can clean up and then Dax can start on whatever he needs to be doing."

Julia looked up at her friends. A year ago she would have had no one to back her up or help her out, and now, she had over a dozen people. She wanted to cry at how amazing it was, but honestly there was no time. "Can Brandon get me into Dockside?" She looked at Leah.

"Let me find out." She got busy texting him as Julia went on.

"Let's have everyone meet there whenever they can." Her phone went off and when she glanced down, she saw it was Wes.

Wes:

I'm on my way to Dockside. What are you planning?

Julia:

I'll meet you there and we can talk.

She stood. "I've gotta go. Wes is on his way there and I want to be there when he arrives. Tell Brandon, nevermind."

"I'll head over about thirty minutes behind you," Avery said.

She waved and headed out.

In her car, she took several deep breaths as she drove to the other side of town. She wasn't sure how Wes was going to take the fact that she was organizing this, but she wasn't willing to sit by and watch his dreams go up in smoke.

Literally.

When she pulled in, there were a few other cars and trucks already there. She recognized Dax's, telling her that Wes's brother was already there ready to do whatever he needed to help. She found Wes inside, talking once again to the fire chief. When he spotted her, he took five long strides until he landed in front of her, his hands landing on her hips.

"I hated waking up without you." He nuzzled her neck. "It made an already unbearable day worse."

She smoothed his hair with her hand. "I was busy trying to fix that unbearable day."

His mouth stopped moving on her neck. "What do you mean you were fixing it?"

"Well not fixing it per se, but finding a way to fix it."

"There's nothing you can do." He was no longer touching her and his eyes were darker than she'd ever seen them.

No, that's wrong, she'd seen them dark the day she told him she was leaving him.

"I figure if you can get approval from the insurance company to go ahead and start working, we could get going on this today, or maybe tomorrow, at the latest."

"I already talked to them this morning and an adjuster is coming out now, but it will be ten working days before I have the money."

"That's where I come in. I have the money and we can start now." She held her breath and waited for the backlash.

"You want to give me the money to fix this?" There was no anger in his voice. It was more like wonder.

"Technically, it will be a loan, since you are getting money from the insurance company, but, if I had to give it to you, I would."

"Why?"

"Because I realized something last night. I love you and I want us to be a couple, and couples do things to help each other out. This," she indicated the restaurant, "is who you are and it's what makes you happy. I would give every penny I have to make sure you were able to keep it."

He didn't say anything, only stared at her. There were other people milling around, so when he pulled her into a quiet corner of the room, she wasn't surprised.

"Each day you do something that blows me away, and this is no different. You make me want to be better. Do more." He looked down at the floor between them. "I'm broke." He left it there like it was news to her.

"First, do you think I didn't know that? I'm a pretty smart person, and even before I found out from Avery that you spent everything you had on this place, I knew you had to be living day-to-day until you started turning an actual profit. Which, if I had to guess, will be soon based on how busy this place is."

"Two more weeks and the start-up costs would be covered."

"See? Secondly, do you think I give a flying fuck if you have money? That's not me and never has been. But guess what? I do have money. Plenty of it, and I want to use it to help the man I love."

"Why do you sound so angry about it?" He was grinning and his eyes were no longer dark.

"Because I don't want you to be all *I am man, hear me roar* and not take what I am offering. Especially, because it's a genuine offer that is coming from a place of love."

"Like you, I consider myself a fairly smart person. Although, I did have a few days where I mixed that up."

She gave him a confused look.

"We'll get to that later. I love you, Lia, and I love that you want to loan me your money so that I can start the process of fixing this place early. I hate thinking that my employees are going to have to go without pay for maybe two weeks, if not longer." He grabbed her hands in his. "So I accept."

She pursed her lips and furrowed her brow at him. "Is this a trick?"

Laughing, he lowered his lips to hers. "No trick. I know a good deal when I hear it." He kissed her, his lips teasing hers for only a few seconds. "Come on, let's go see what's happening."

Holding hands, they walked back to where all the people were. She was elated that he was game for her idea, and hoped this was just the start of them compromising.

Chapter 17

Wes looked around and watched as all his friends and family worked to clean up the mess the fire had made. His own mom was there, and incredibly so was Julia's. Joanne, Julia's mom, had said that this was what family did.

Family.

He wanted to be a family with Julia.

Both of them together, and maybe someday, kids.

Would she want kids?

Had all the years that passed changed her mine?

When they'd been young they'd always talked about having a family someday. But it was always way in the future. Like when they turned twenty-five.

He laughed to himself. Twenty-five felt like a hundred years ago. At thirty-four he knew that he could have kids well into the future, but he also knew that women couldn't. He read enough, and watched enough news to know that at thirty-four, the prime pregnancy years were over. They were definitely going to have to have a conversation soon if they even wanted to contemplate kids.

Tony was walking toward him, Logan hot on his heels.

Logan was just the guy he wanted to talk to. "Hey Logan, did you meet, Jimmy?" Jimmy had heard about the fire on TV and came over to check things out. He immediately volunteered to help saying it was this or sitting at home and maybe getting into trouble.

"Yeah," he looked behind him to where Jimmy was working, "good kid. Hard worker."

"He has ambitions of being either a photographer or maybe a graphic designer. I thought you might be able to, I don't know, mentor him?"

"Absolutely! I'd love to."

"Great, I'll give him your number."

"I'll just go talk to him." Logan walked away, going directly to where Jimmy was standing.

Tony shook his head. "When Logan wants something he just does it, but every other second of the day, it's like he's in slow motion."

"I've noticed that."

"We need to talk about your security here."

"I don't have any security here."

"That's what we need to talk about. You need a system, Wes. If you had one, right now we would know who started this fire."

"I don't have the extra money to put one in right now."

"Yes you do." Julia came up behind him. "Wes, Tony is right. This is important, and not only that, but you have Sabrina, who sometimes closes, and it's just her and a couple of waitresses. That's not safe for them."

He turned to her. "I can't take your money for this. It'll be months before I can pay you back."

"So what? This is important. What if it was me working here?"

"I'd want you to be safe."

"Then you should want the same for all your employees."

"While you make a good point, I don't love any of them."

"If you love me, you'll do this."

He sighed. "Tony, tell me what I need."

Julia patted his ass as he and Tony walked away. He knew she was right, but he hated wasting her money.

Hours later, it was just the two of them left. The place had been aired out, the back wall of the kitchen gutted and everything that could be cleaned was cleaned. It had been two long days of work and Wes wanted nothing but a bed with Julia next to him.

But first, he wanted to talk to her. If he waited until they were home, talk would be the last thing on his mind.

"Remember when we were talking about houses and you said you want to live in a lake house?"

"Yeah."

He went for broke and said, "I can't afford that. Right now."

She tilted her head to the side. "Okay. I'm pretty sure everything that has gone on the last two days has made me aware of that."

"I'm saying that I know you want a house, and I want a house too, but if you are with me, it's going to be a while until I can afford it."

She ran a hand over her face. "Okay let's take this one thing at a time. We've covered that all your money is tied up in this place. I get that, and don't give a shit. Wes, I have money. If we want to buy a house, I can contribute. And even if I'm the only one contributing, who cares." She shook her head. "Now what's this if you are with me crap? Do you want to break up?"

"No, the opposite of that. I want to be together. Forever hopefully, but I don't want to bring you down." If he was going to do this, he might as well go all in. "You are the love of my life, Lia. And after all these years, we made our way back to each other, and that is a miracle. But, just like you want to give me all the things I want in life, I want to do the same for you. Only I can't. I have nothing to offer."

She sighed and stepped closer to him. "I love you, Wes and I want a future with you too. But let me ask you something. If it was me coming into this relationship with no money because I had reached for my dream, would you care?"

"No." He shook his head. "I wouldn't give a shit."

"Exactly. We are a team and we have to do this together. Sure now, I have more money, but who's to say that'll be the case in five or ten years? This place is amazing, and eventually, you will start making money. And when that happens, if you want to pay all the bills, more power to you."

He smiled and ran a hand down her cheek. "I love you so much. I'm not even sure how I made it through the last fourteen years without you."

"You'll never have to find out again. I'm not going anywhere." She leaned in and kissed him. "Let's stop worrying about who pays for what and start enjoying all the time we have together. We missed so much, let's not miss anymore."

"You're so amazing and I have no idea what I did in life to deserve you. But, it doesn't matter, because I'm not giving you up." His lips lowered to hers. He was overwhelmed with emotions as he devoured her mouth. He needed her, and he wasn't willing to wait until they got home.

His lips trailed to her ear. "I need you."

"I need you too." She dropped her head back giving him complete access to her neck. "Here. Fuck me here."

Grinning against her skin, he slid his tongue out and licked her ear. "Great minds think alike."

She pushed him away, his back hitting the bar. He watched as she pulled her shirt over her head and then pushed her shorts down her legs. Slowly she unclasped her bra, sliding it down her arms. He was salivating at the sight of her breasts. They were his new favorite thing, and he didn't think he'd ever get enough of them.

As she slipped her panties from her body, he ripped his own shirt from his body. After kicking off his shoes, he hurriedly pulled off his pants, taking his boxers with them.

"On the bar," he told her.

She raised an eyebrow. "Weren't you the one who only recently complained about the counter at Dax and Avery's?"

He stalked toward her. "That was before I had you. Now I understand the need to have sex whenever and wherever we are." He was right on top of her, his chest rubbing up against her breasts. "Up on the bar, Lia."

She bit her bottom lip, but did as he asked, and climbed onto the bar. The lights were out in the place so if anyone happened to look into the front window, they wouldn't see much. He moved in closer, once she was seated on the bar. Running his fingers down her leg, he watched her shiver under his touch.

After spreading her legs with his shoulders, he leaned in and kissed her inner thigh.

"Wes." Her voice was hoarse, and when he looked up, he saw she had closed her eyes and her mouth was hanging open.

Smiling, he moved in even closer, licking up her center. Her groan vibrated through her whole body making his already hard cock grow more. He began devouring her, and because he couldn't stop himself, he lifted a hand and cupped one breast. His thumb ran over the hard nipple as his tongue speared into her. She cried out as an orgasm pulsed through her body.

"Stop, stop," she panted out, grabbing his hair and yanking his mouth off of her. "No more please."

"There's going to be more, so you better get ready." He picked her up from the bar and walked over to a table. The bar was too high for sex, but the table was the perfect height. Finding his pants, he pulled out a condom, opened it and rolled it down his dick. Pushing her legs up, he moved between them. With no warning, he pushed deep inside her.

"Fuck!" she swore.

"Hold on, baby." His fingers dug deeper into her hip with each thrust. She was so tight around him. Nothing had ever felt so good. Her boobs shook with every push of his body against hers and he couldn't seem to take his eyes off them. Leaning forward, he took a nipple into his mouth, her hands cradling his head against her chest as he did.

He felt himself climbing toward release, but held back long enough for her to come. When her body shook in orgasm, he tensed up and let himself pump into her.

Both of them were breathing heavily as they stared into the other's eyes. "I can't believe we had sex in the restaurant."

"This is definitely a violation of the health code." He smiled and backed up, pulling out of her.

"Don't make me laugh."

He shrugged. "You know once Tony installs those cameras, there is no way we can do this."

"Listen, I love you, but don't ever plan on filming us having sex. It's at the top of my list of things I will not do."

He threw her clothes to her. "What are the other things on this list?"

"Don't worry, I'll tell you if they ever come up."

Once they were both dressed, Wes locked up and they left for home. He drove, and almost three minutes in, Julia was sound asleep, her head leaning against the door.

He turned the music down so it wouldn't wake her and drove quietly to his apartment. When he parked, she was still asleep. He tried to wake her, but she only moaned sleepily. He went to her door and opened it carefully, picking her up in his arms. Inside his apartment, he moved through until he was in his room, where he placed her gently on the bed. Pulling her shoes off, he dropped them to the floor before covering her up. He was dirty from a day of work and desperately wanted a shower. As he stripped off his clothes, she stirred on the bed.

"What are you doing?"

"Go back to sleep. I'm gonna take a quick shower."

"Hurry."

He walked out of the room, closing the door behind him. He showered fast, wanting badly to be in bed with Julia in his arms. The time he spent with her never seemed to be enough. It was like she was his new addiction.

Only he had no desire to purge her from his body.

When he entered his room, he found her still asleep. After finding boxers, he slid into bed next to her, wrapping her in his arms.

"I love you," he whispered against her ear.

The fire had thrown them for a loop, and it could have been a relationship breaker. Instead, he'd thrown out all his notions about what he'd thought to be normal in relationships. He loved her, and it didn't matter if she had more money or if he did. She'd made him see that love was the most important thing.

That when you were in love, you shared and compromised.

And loving her was what he was meant to do.

Chapter 18

Julia couldn't believe the progress that had been made on Dockside in only four days. She'd had to go to her actual job during the day, and because Wes was worried she would tire herself out, he wouldn't let her come help at night. In fact, he was done each night by seven so they had time to spend together.

But, now it was Wednesday and she'd told him she was stopping in. whether he wanted her to or not. Stepping in the kitchen, she could see how much had been done.

"Julia," Avery said, walking toward her, "it's about time you came in."

"This place looks amazing. It almost looks as if it's finished?"

"It is finished," Addison said, coming up beside her. "Those guys over there," she pointed to where Wes was standing with three other men, "those are the inspectors. If they give it the okay, Wes can open tomorrow."

"Seriously? He never mentioned anything."

"He wanted it to be a surprise," Avery said. "He's worked his ass off this week."

"I can see that."

"I finished up the security system a few hours ago and Tony is currently testing it, because I'm dead on my feet," Addison said.

"You should go home," Julia told her. "Your body needs to rest."

"I'm heading there now."

As she walked away, Avery asked, "Things seem good with you and Wes."

She smiled. "They're crazy good. I can only imagine how hard this has been for him, but instead of getting down, he's kept his head up and we've worked through it."

She was so proud of how he'd handled the whole thing. She knew that going through addiction, and then therapy, had helped him tremendously and taught him how to deal with his problems, but she'd never seen anyone come out the other side so...well balanced.

"You know you made this happen right? He never would have been able to open so soon if it hadn't been for you."

She crossed her arms and looked across the room at Wes. "He would have figured something out. He's the most remarkable man I know."

"The Lange men are both pretty fantastic."

"Do you believe in fate?"

"I never did, but when I met Dax, that all changed. Our connection was immediate and strong. Call it fate, or love at first sight, or anything else, it doesn't matter. All that matters is that when you find the person who is your other half, you hold on for dear life and never let them go."

"I wish I wouldn't have let him go fourteen years ago."

"You had to, Julia. The likelihood of you making it back then with him addicted to drugs still, is slim to none. You needed to find your own ways."

She watched as the group of men, including Wes split up. He looked over to where she was and waved as he walked toward her.

"I'll talk to you later," Avery said as Wes got closer.

"Hi," he said and pulled her into his body. His grin was the biggest she'd ever seen.

"Someone's happy."

"I get to open tomorrow. Four days of business is all I lost." He kissed her hard. "This is the best day."

She held on as he spun her around. "This is great news."

"We need to celebrate. I'm taking you out tonight. Go home, put on something sexy, and short, and I'll pick you up in an hour."

She loved his good mood. "Deal. But only if you wear something equally as sexy." She kissed him and then turned and walked away.

"What's sexy for guys?" he called out after her.

"You'll figure it out!"

She drove home and found her mom eating dinner when she walked inside.

"Hey, mom, how was your day?"

"Good. I went by Dockside for a few hours this morning and then Kelly and I had lunch." Kelly was Wes and Dax's mom.

Not that she cared if they became friends, actually it would be better. But when they'd been teenagers, she'd always felt that her parents didn't like Kelly. "It's nice to see you getting along."

"We always got along, but when you and Wes first started dating, we wanted to keep our distance in case you broke up."

"Ahh, that makes sense. I guess." She gave her mom a *whatever you say* look. "I have to go get ready. Wes is taking me out."

"Have fun."

She took a fast shower, opting not to wash her hair and then picked out her skimpiest dress. It wasn't even all that skimpy, but it was the only one she had that wasn't a plain black, boring dress. It was blue and made of a thin material that showed every line or wrinkle underneath. That meant wearing underwear was out. Unfortunately, she had to wear a bra or the whole world would see her nipples.

After she was dressed, she added a few curls to her hair and darkened her eyeliner for a sexier look. Digging through her closet, she found her highest pair of summer heels. She couldn't remember the last time she'd worn them, but the moment she'd seen them in the store, she had to have them.

They made her feel tall and powerful.

And sexy.

She was switching her money and cards to a small handbag, when she heard a car pull up. She finished quickly and made it to the door, just as he knocked. When she opened the door, he was standing in front of her wearing a suit, but without a tie.

"That's a pretty sexy look." She bit her bottom lip.

"I've changed my mind." His eyes traveled down her body and back up again. "I think we should stay in."

Raising both her arms, she spun around. "Sexy enough for you?"

"Maybe too sexy." He reached for her, but instead of touching her, he ran a finger over the material of her dress. "What do you have on under this?"

"Wouldn't you like to know." She winked and stepped past him, shutting the door behind her.

He groaned loudly. "Are you trying to kill me?"

"Oh no, I'd never want to do that." She walked in front of him, and she knew the moment he realized she wasn't wearing much under her dress.

"Holy fuck."

She added a little extra sway to her hips to grab his attention. Not that she needed to. He was beside her in a second.

"You are a wicked, wicked woman." He opened the door of the truck for her.

"Can you give me a boost up?" She lifted one foot to the truck, making her dress ride up higher. She could have easily gotten in by herself, but if he helped, his hands would have to touch her bare legs and that would drive him even more insane.

"God, I love you," he said as he slid his hand up her bent leg. Maybe she should have rethought this. Now that his hands were on her, she wasn't sure she wanted him to stop. He leaned his body into hers, his other hand coming around her stomach. She felt him hard and pressing into her back. "You are so fucking sexy." He bit down on her earlobe.

She dropped her head against his chest and tried not to moan. "Maybe we should just stay here."

That seemed to snap him out of his lust. "No. I'm showing you off. Behave." He gently pushed her up and into the truck. She laughed as he shut the door, and while he walked around the truck, she buckled her seatbelt.

"Where are we going?" She asked when he got in and started the engine.

"I thought it might be fun to head into Woodridge and try out that new Italian place. Dax mentioned it to me a while ago and it sounds good."

"Works for me."

The drive was short and soon they were seated at a table in the corner.

"Holy crap it smells amazing in here," she said as she opened her menu. "I feel like I want one of everything."

"Get whatever you want." He was also looking at his menu.

"Hey Wes," he looked over the top of his menu at her, "I love you." Seeing him across from her just made her want to tell him.

"I love you too." He set his menu down. "I wanted to bring you out tonight because I feel like we never got to do this right. We never dated. I never got to woo you."

"That's what this is about?" She set her menu aside and inclined her head. "You do remember that we did all that years ago, right?"

"But it's not the same." He looked so serious. "We are different people now and these two people should get all the things that everyone else gets, not just stolen moments after work or you sitting at the bar waiting for me."

"I like sitting at the bar waiting for you. I love Dockside and I want to be as much a part of it as you'll let me." She bit her lip unsure of if she should say more. In the end she decided to just put it all out there. "I don't want it to be just your place. I want it to be our place." She hoped he understood what she was saying.

"You have a job. One you love."

"And I'm not leaving that, right now. I love what I do, but I'd love to someday segway into just doing the group therapy. And when I do that, I will have a lot of extra time to be at the restaurant. Where you will be."

"I don't want you to give anything up for me."

"Listen to me, Wes. I am doing what I want. I gave you up once, and I'm not doing it again. You are what I want. And I don't care if you work twenty-four hours a day and I have to sit there the whole time watching you."

Wes let out a breath and started laughing. Then he pushed back from his chair. "Come with me."

"What?" She looked up at him questioning what he was doing.

"Please come with me." He held out his hand.

Standing, she put her hand in his and followed him through the restaurant and out the door. "Where are we going?" She was laughing now because she was so confused.

"Just don't ask any questions." They walked all the way to his truck where he opened the door and helped her inside.

Buckling her seatbelt, she questioned him again when he was seated. "What happened to dinner?"

He looked at her with a huge smile on his face. "You'll see soon enough." He drove them in the direction of Cedarville and somehow she stopped herself from asking a billion questions. When he pulled up in front of Dockside, she was even more confused.

"What are we doing here?" He gave her a sly smile and then got out of the truck.

She started laughing hysterically as he ran around the front of the truck and then opened her door. Helping her out, he took her hand in his as they walked into the building. He kept going all the way through the restaurant and out onto the deck. He'd flipped the lights on before they walked out and the whole outside was lit up with those small Christmas lights. She'd never been out there at night, so she'd never noticed them.

"Lia, I love you. I've loved you since I was fourteen and started to understand what love was. I never want to be without you again." Gripping her hands in his, he lowered to one knee in front of her. She gasped as he pulled a ring box from his pocket. "You said you wanted to give me my dreams, well you're my dream. I would give up everything else if it meant I got you. Please do me the honor of being my wife."

Tears were streaming down her cheeks. He'd brought her there to propose. And he had a ring. "When did you get this?" She looked down at the ring in the box. It looked old, almost antique.

"It was my great, great grandmother's. My mom gave it to me when I was eighteen, and I've been saving it for you, ever since."

She dropped to her knees in front of him which wasn't easy in heels and a dress. Nodding fast, she wiped her eyes. "Yes. Yes, yes, yes." She grabbed his face in her hands and kissed him. "A million times yes!"

He fumbled, pulling the ring out of the box and sliding it on her finger. "I've been carrying this ring with me since the morning after you barged in here to yell at me. This was the place we reconnected, so this is the place I wanted to propose."

"It's perfect." She knew she was smiling like a crazy person, but she couldn't help it. Wes had proposed to her. She was getting married. He helped her stand, and under the moonlight, they held each other. She laid her head on his shoulder and it was almost like they were dancing.

"I don't know how you feel, but I don't want to wait to get married. I feel like I have already waited forever."

She lifted her head. "I feel the same way."

His lips touched hers. "Good, then I have an idea. What would you think about this Saturday, right here?"

Her eyes went wide. "You want to get married this Saturday? As in three days from now?"

"Yeah, but only if you want to."

She closed her eyes, took a deep breath and answered honestly. "Yes. I will marry you Saturday."

"Woohoo!" he picked her up and spun her around, both of them laughing.

She was overwhelmed with love. Love for Wes and their future together.

Those two young kids, who had fallen in love almost twenty years ago, had finally found their way back to each other. She still wasn't sure about fate or soulmates, but she knew with every beat of her heart that she and Wes were meant to be.

The only man she'd ever loved was going to be the man she had the privilege of loving for the rest of her life.

And that was just fine by her.

Also by Bree Kraemer
The Only Series
Only By His Touch
Only With Trust
If Only
Only You
Only For Love
Cedarville Novels
An Unexpected Home
Capturing Us
Choosing You
Better Together
A Chance Worth Taking
Forever Starts Here
After All These Years
Won't Let You Down
Say When
Something to Lose
Finally Home
Friends & Brothers
Sky High Love
Bridge To Love
When It's Love
Rockstar Romance
The Right Note
Pick Me
Christmas Novella
Light Me Up
DecorHATE for the Holidays
The Beckmeyer Family
Hooked
Sparked
Shocked
Kneaded
Valley Falls Strikers
Late Tackle
First Touch
Give & Go
Narrowing the Angle

He's a Keeper
Ground Rule
Walk Off
Sacrifice Bunt
Grand Slam (April 2023)

www.ingramcontent.com/pod-product-compliance
Lightning Source LLC
Chambersburg PA
CBHW031458160726
47994CB00005B/2097